D1030925

Parson John

Parson John

A Saga of the Winning of the West

by
BERNARD PALMER

Second Edition

WM. B. EERDMANS PUBLISHING COMPANY
Grand Rapids   1943   Michigan

PARSON JOHN
by BERNARD PALMER

FOREWORD

This story is offered humbly, with the prayer that its message might find a place in your heart. The original Parson John, who was the author's grandfather, was preaching and ministering in Western Nebraska at the turn of the century. Many of the events depicted in the following pages actually happened to him. All of them could have. He was a very ordinary individual, possessing as his only claim to greatness, a fierce, unquenchable love of God.

Parson John wasn't unique. Churches of every denomination throughout the broad expanse of our midwest had his prototype in the pulpit. They were devout men of God who, armed only with the Bible and their unbounding faith, went out into a hostile country alone, and conquered. They were cursed, and fought, and hated wherever they went, because men feared the Gospel they preached. Today those men are largely forgotten, their names lost in the musty records of the churches they served. And very probably that is the way they would have it; for they cared only in laying the foundation so that their children, and their children's children might have the opportunity to know Jesus.

THE AUTHOR

Parson John

Chapter 1

JOHN WOODRING paced nervously across the thick velvet rug in the reception room, to the window. He wasn't a big man, but his shiny, ill-fitting suit and gangling arms gave the illusion of size. His face was lean and earnest, far older than his twenty-three years. And his fiery thatch of hair lent credence to the suggestion of a smoldering temper that was telegraphed by his eyes.

A warm Nebraska sun was whispering to the trees and grass and birds, like a maestro drawing out the brilliance of a great symphony. The cottonwoods and box elders just outside the window were splashed with green, and the early flowers were pushing into bud. Cattle on the range would be shedding their winter hair, and rounding sleek and fat on the newly-greened prairies, while the season's first calves were finding the world a new and exciting place. It was spring, and all of nature was blossoming.

He glanced up the little stairway to the right, and at the door towards the back of the room. The Bishop might appear from either place, unannounced. The thought frightened him, for the Bishop had always been a symbol of the Church to him. John held him very much in awe, the same as he did President McKinley and the King of England.

He turned and surveyed himself in the mirror on the wall. He had never thought much about his appearance before, but now it mattered a great deal to him. His hair had grown down to the nape of his neck, curling up at his coat collar, and his fingernails were dirty and uncut. His clothes

9

were almost as shabby as his education, and his manners would scarcely be acceptable to one who lived in such a place as this. Suddenly he wanted to run away, but of course that was impossible.

John's eyes swept the richly furnished room once more. There was nothing like it in the hills of Missouri where he first began to preach. The families on his circuit huddled together in log cabins and shacks that were far too small for their numbers; and his wages, more often than not, had been a sack of beans and a side of salt pork. It was strange, but money never seemed to work its way into the Ozarks. At home there had always been plenty to eat, even tho the variety was skimpy at times, but there was seldom any money for clothes or books. His father hadn't believed in 'book larnin'.

"I never saw it help a man raise bigger 'taters," he used to say, when asked why John and his sister didn't come to school. "And I never seen it fetch a bigger ear of corn. It's a lot of tom foolishness, that's what it is."

It had been almost three years ago that John felt the call to the ministry. He had been a gangling, raw-boned kid, far too busy building a reputation as the toughest fighter in the hills, to have any time for the church; until a chance visit by a wandering evangelist re-awakened the religious life of the Woodring family. He would never forget the day that he told his folks. They were all gathered about the breakfast table, and his father had just finished reading, haltingly, from the big Bible for their family worship, when John said, "Paw, I'm going to be a preacher." For the first time in his life he saw tears in his father's eyes.

The next morning when he came down to breakfast there was a copy of Hitchcock's Bible Analysis on the table beside his plate. It wasn't until a year later that he learned that they had mortgaged their best cow to buy it for him.

Those first three years had been hard. There were times when he worked from dawn until dusk pulling stumps or cutting hay with a scythe, only to come home and study until the first timid rays of sunlight pushed above the hills. Even when he had enough of studying, there had been another hurdle to leap; tortuous days at the Conference where the Bishops bombarded him with theological questions for hours on end, and finally had him preach a sermon for their critical ears. Weeks had followed before he learned that he had survived the ordeal and was permitted to preach for the small, but active denomination.

He rode the circuit tirelessly, teaching the Gospel of Christ, preaching funerals, and performing marriages; eating greasy, poorly cooked meals, and sleeping on the floor or in haymows wherever he happened to be at nightfall. These folks gave their best to him, but often their best was little better than nothing at all. John smiled a little in spite of his nervousness. He had worn out one good saddle horse, and had almost worn out his stomach on that job.

If it hadn't been for Martha he would probably still be preaching in the Ozarks. He had met her, and had fallen in love with her, at prayer meeting in one of the school houses on his circuit almost a year ago. She was a dark, brown-haired maiden about his own age. Her soft, limpid eyes could melt the anger that ebbed and flowed, unconquerable, within his heart; or change in a twinkling, when his spirits were low, to goad him to renewed effort. Her formal education had been as meagre as his own. But she had that rare foresight and knowledge that sometimes is bestowed upon a woman, and she served as a balance-wheel for his otherwise unpredictable temperament. Martha was a fine, Christian girl. His job would never pay enough to permit them to marry, so he made application to the Methodists for a charge outside the Ozark mountains. They accepted him, and gave him a church at Hanridge, some two hundred and twenty-five miles west of Omaha, in Nebraska. He and Martha had planned on being married as soon as he was settled, but now that had all been blasted.

There was a step on the stairs, and John turned from the window. The Bishop took his hand warmly and asked him to sit down — all his self-consciousness vanished.

"I suppose you are wondering why I sent for you." Bishop King dropped comfortably into a huge chair. He was a short, round little man whose jowls bounced and shook when he talked. He was meticulously dressed, but, if he noticed his visitor's clothes and shaggy hair, he made no sign. "Tell me, what's been your problem out at Hanridge?"

"The church was going strong when I got there," John launched into the story without a trace of the fear that he had dreaded. "I reckon it's the kind of a place I always wanted to work in. But there was a tol'able lot of things that wasn't right, things I just couldn't stomach.

"The town was plumb full of filth and graft. Saloon-keepers and gamblers did as they pleased. Ever so often they were arrested and brought before the police judge. And, just as often, they paid their fines and walked out. The city officials had made it quite a way to collect taxes and graft.

"It wasn't ary twenty-four hours till I found out what was going on. I laid plans to get the congregation behind me, so we could start a campaign to clean up the town. I reckon I never even thought they wouldn't want their town cleaned up.

"Sunday morning a large crowd came in to the new frame church. When I came over for Sunday school the street was just lined with the town folks' carriages, and the buggies and saddle horses of the farmers. I'll tell you I was right pleased to see so many there.

"I didn't preach a regular sermon that day. Maybe I should have, but when I saw so many out I couldn't pass up the opportunity. I told them I was new there, and just wanted to talk to them for a few minutes about their town. I spoke about the clean homes and streets, and the fine looking youngsters playing in the yards. Then I mentioned the town's short-comings.

"Folks straightened up and looked at each other, and Oscar Johnson, he was on the town council, banged his cane on the floor.

"I told them how some of the men in our town, in our very own church, wouldn't ary be seen in a saloon or gambling house. Yet they had whiskey in their homes, and frequented the gambling dens at every opportunity.

"By this time every one was getting riled up. One old fellow, who must've liked his hot toddy and a snifter or two of brandy on cold mornings, got up and stomped outside. Wives was watching their husbands like they was trying to figure out just who I was talking about.

"I went to the door to shake hands with them as they went home, but they were sure temper-headed. The women barely nodded when they walked by, and the men acted like I wasn't even there. I reckon they must've been touched on a sore spot, the way they squirmed.

"The next night when I moseyed out for a walk I saw a light in the church, and a row of buggies tied to the hitching rail out front. So I went inside.

"The Oscar Johnson I was telling you about was talking in front of a tol'able big crowd of men, and the old fellow who had walked out on the sermon was sitting beside him. His face turned red when he saw me. I reckoned what was up, and my blood started to boil." John looked at the Bishop, but the latter made no move to interrupt.

" 'If this meeting's about my sermon yesterday I reckon I'll just stay,' I said. They didn't much act like they wanted me, but I went down the center aisle right to the front seat.

" 'Parson, it's not that we don't like you,' Johnson explained. 'But this here town is a good enough place, as towns go. You said so yourself. The thing is, if we don't have a little amusement for the boys, they'll all go somewhere's else to trade.'

" 'Besides, the church hasn't got no call prying into a body's private affairs,' the fellow who owned the grocery store busted in. 'I got a bottle of whiskey in my pantry, just for my indigestion, mind you, but I don't like being made a public example.'

"They all agreed with that, and a big man I'd never seen before got up. 'Fact of the matter is, Parson,' he said, 'we just decided that everything'd be fine here, if we could only get together with you, so you wouldn't preach no more sermons we don't like.'

"I got up and walked over to the pulpit and back again. I must have been mad by that time, because I could almost feel my forehead turning red, and my face getting hot. 'It's all right if I preach nice, sugary sermons that please the wo-

men and pat the kids on the heads, is that it? But you don't
want any thing that's apt to hurt, do you?' I said. 'You want
me to be careful I don't step on no one's toes!'

" 'Well, I wouldn't put it that way,' he answered. 'We
don't want to interfere with you atall. We want you to
preach just the way you want to preach, with—er—a reserva-
tions.'

" 'Gentlemen,' I said, 'there's one way I'll preach in Hanridge, or anywhere's alse, and only one way. I've got to be
allowed to preach when I want to, where I want to, and
about who I want to!'

" 'You don't have to decide tonight,' they told me. 'Better
think it over till morning, anyway.'

"But I was so mad I packed up and left."

The Bishop got up and stepped closer to John, leaning
back against the table. "I can see your point of view, and I
do admire your stand," he said. "There's times when a man's
got to stand up for what he believes, no matter what it may
cost him. But, an older, more experienced man might have
accomplished his purpose without being forced to face such
a situation."

He eyed John critically. "I want to speak to you as a
friend, son. You have the character, the personality, and the
faith to make a great minister; but, like all of us, you have
got some things that need the tempering of experience and
age. There are times when you can't blast a bad condition
out of a town. Sometimes you must fight slowly and carefully, gaining a friend here, and an ally there, until you
are able to present a force capable of succeeding. I think
that your own uncontrollable temper is your greatest
enemy."

"I reckon that's right, Bishop King."

"Don't take this as a rebuke, Brother Woodring, but rather as a lesson for the future." He pulled out a drawer in the library table and got a letter from it.

"This just came today," he said. "It concerns a field in the western part of the state. They're desperately in need of a worker, a consecrated worker like yourself. I understand that the town has a population of about four hundred and fifty, and is without a church of any kind. It's a marvelous opportunity. Would you like to try it?"

John's face lighted. "I sure would."

So a new minister went to Hanridge, and John boarded a train for Regina Springs, in the heart of the sandhills, about twenty miles north and east of North Platte.

Chapter 2

THE only hills that John had ever known were the cool, green, tree-covered Ozarks, where the people were backward, and somewhat reticent about strangers until one got to know them and gained their trust. Then they showed a friendliness and fellowship unequaled anywhere else. He had missed that during his short stay at Hanridge. He missed the rivers and creeks that were full of fish, and the squirrels and coons and 'possums that he loved to hunt so well. It would be nice to live in such surroundings again.

Regina Springs was a little town; that may have been the reason that he looked forward, so keenly, to working and preaching there. A minister could accomplish things in small places, where the neighbors were few and the distances long. He could vision the wide streets, and clean white homes with children playing in the yards. The stores would be in the center of the town around a square, with, perhaps, a little park in the middle.

The train ride was a long one, and John chafed at the numerous delays. The antiquated engine wheezed and groaned as it jerked the cars along, like a small boy leading a protesting cow to water. At every stop the local lingered unhurriedly, and John kept looking out the window, searching the horizon for the hills and forests that he expected to find.

He was eager to be at work, justifying himself before Bishop King. For all the Bishop's kindliness, John stung under

17

the gentle rebuke. Nothing less than establishing the church quickly would redeem himself in his own eyes.

The train bucked and screeched to a halt, and he leaned forward once more to stare out of the window. He could scarcely believe what his eyes recorded, it was so different, so barren, so vast. A rolling wedge of naked prairie stretched before him. The hills were little more than mounds of sand, and as alike as a quarter's worth of marbles rolled out onto the floor. If there were any trees, or signs of life, he couldn't see them. The sun had dropped behind the hills, and soft, tangent rays of light were struggling vainly against the growing darkness. For a moment he felt so insignificant and alone that it panicked him.

On the other side of the train was a handful of loading pens, with a grimy, dust-laden cowboy tending the cattle that were awaiting shipment to the east. Up the track was a run-down shack that John took to be the depot, and a jumble of dirty, unpainted buildings with gaudy, pretentious false fronts that hid the squalid framework. Hopes had bloomed high when the buildings were first erected; but, through the years, sand and wind had blasted away the paint, drying the siding until it cracked, and loosening the windows that once fit tight. The houses and stores looked as though they had been dropped onto the prairie without purpose or plan, to desecrate the spot on which they set.

"Is that — is that Regina Springs?" he managed to ask the conductor.

"Yep, that's her! The toughest little town east of Cheyenne." He looked John over quizzically. "Say, young fellow, what are you aiming to do in a place like this?"

"I'm the new minister," he said pridefully.

The conductor looked at him and laughed. "Well, Parson, you sure got a job cut out for yourself."

John gathered up his delapidated suitcase, and the pasteboard box that contained a few of his books, and got off the train. He stood for a moment, with his arms full of packages, and his hat shoved back on his head, staring bewilderedly about. The wide main street was hub-deep in shifting sand.

"I'd sure be beholden to you, if you'd tell me of a place to stay, and get some victuals. I'm a stranger here."

The agent sauntered out on the platform. He was a small man, with shifty eyes and a bushy, black moustache that gave his mouth a fierce quality. "I know where there's a *good* room," he winked broadly. "And you won't have to go far to find a little game or some stuff to wet your whistle."

"I get what you're driving at," John retorted. "I'm the new minister here."

The agent threw back his head and laughed uproariously. "The last Parson didn't only stay till the next train come through. You'll be comfortable right here in the station till then."

"I reckon you don't understand. I aim to stay."

"Oh you do, do you? Well, maybe some of us'll have something to say about that. This here town is a rip snorter. We got no need for preaching and the like of that. You'd better just get right back on this next train while you got your duds packed. Might save both us and you a sight of trouble."

"I don't scare easy," John answered, keeping his voice and his temper down.

"Well, if that's the case you can probably get a room up to Belle Williams'," he grinned broadly, as though it were some huge joke. "They might put you up for a spell."

John thanked him and went on up the street to the house he had pointed out. It was a big, ramshackle building that looked as though it might collapse if someone leaned heavily on it. The front porch sagged in the middle like a sailor's hammock, and the shutters in front were hanging from a single hinge. But at that it was in better condition than most of the other houses in Regina Springs; for all the windows were in and had the screens on, and there was still enough paint on the clapboards so that one could tell it had once been white. There were ten or fifteen saddle horses crowded along the hitching rail at one side of the house, and the tin pan clatter of an off key piano sounded from within. John looked about, queerly.

A slatternly, faded landlady came to the door and stared at him critically. He looked like a drummer that had just started out on his first trip. A lock or two of red hair had escaped his hat and hung down over his forehead, and his pock-marked face took on a pinkish hue under her bland gaze.

"What do you want?" she grated.

He was somewhat taken aback by her brusque manner. "Why I — I'd like a room."

"I can't serve you no supper," she explained gruffly. "We already et, and we don't run no short order house. If you're not here when it's on the table you go hungry."

"That don't matter," John said weakly. After seeing Regina Springs he didn't think that he'd ever be hungry again.

"Well, come along."

He followed her upstairs, and to the far end of the dark hall.

"This here's the room," she said, throwing open the door. It was dirty and small, with an iron bed in one corner, and an old dresser with a cracked mirror in the other.

"It isn't so big, is it?" he said.

"What do you expect for two dollars a week, the Bridal Suite?"

John set his luggage on the floor and paid her two weeks in advance. She was a large, full-figured woman about thirty-five years old. Her thick jowls were splattered carelessly with powder, and each cheek was dabbed with rouge.

"If you eat here it'll cost you five more."

"That suits me fine."

"Now I don't ask no questions of my guests, and I don't expect to answer none. There's only two things I ask you. Don't get drunk in your room, and don't beef to me about what you lose downstairs."

"You don't need to worry about that," he said. "I'm going to be the new minister here."

"A Parson?" she queried, stepping close to him, her eyes as wild as her tousled hair. "Did I hear you right? Did I hear you say you're a Parson?"

"That's right. I'm going to start holding meetings, and when we begin fetching out good crowds we plan on building a church."

"I should've knowed that 'holier than thou' look about you. Well, you can't stay here. This room's not for rent to no Parson."

"I won't pester you none, Sister Williams. I'm awfully tired tonight, and I'd like to stay, at least till morning."

"I should say not. Havin' a Parson sneaking around spying on you," she snorted. "And giving pretty speeches. There won't be none of it at Belle Williams, I can tell you that. Why, the boys would laugh me out of town."

He picked up his suitcase and box and started down the steps, when the door opened and a dowdy, heavily-rouged woman twenty-eight or thirty years old swaggered in. She took off the red fox neckpiece with a flourish, and hung it on a halltree in the corner.

"I hear we got us a new boarder," she smirked.

"He's on his way out, Clara. He's a *preacher*," the landlady said. "We got enough troubles without no preacher causing a fuss."

Clara looked him over, a laugh toying with the corners of her mouth. She looked very much like the landlady, with her thick, painted lips and peroxide bleached hair that fuzzed about her head like the hair of a poodle dog. John took them to be sisters.

"I know all about it, Belle. I heard them talking about him uptown. Why don't you let him stay?" She whispered something to the older woman, and they both laughed.

"Well, come on upstairs, Parson. Clara says to let you stay, so I reckon it'll be all right if you stay. You won't be here long, nohow."

John knew now why the station agent had laughed as he sent him out to the boarding house. He prayed, and went to sleep with the clatter of dice, and the rough voices of the gamblers ringing in his ears. The piano was hammered sporadically.

The next morning he overslept and was late for breakfast. He smiled a little when he saw that the table was being cleared, and went out the front door without speaking to anyone.

The town was even more squalid than it had seemed the night before. Main street was three blocks long, with stores scattered along its entire length, generously interspersed with vacant lots. A few bedraggled, sleepy teams stood complacently at the hitching rails, and the racks in front of the saloons were full. The Bishop's information had been greatly exaggerated when it said that Regina Springs had a population of four hundred and fifty. It probably would do well to top two hundred on any day but Saturday.

John went into the general store and introduced himself.

"I am glad to see you," the storekeeper replied, thrusting his hand into John's. His voice was thick and heavy with a Bohemian accent. "Come out from what you are doing, Mamma. The Parson is here."

His wife came waddling out of their living quarters at the back of the store, wiping her hands on the hem of a greasy apron. She was a big woman, with a ruddy complexion and coarse features.

"So glad am I that you come, Parson," she said. "Every night we say, 'Please, dear God, do something to make this wicked place decent for our children.' Now you have come to do it, maybe." Then her face flushed as she suddenly remembered her manners. "Excuse me, I am so excite I forget to do my manners. Won't you set awhile?" She hauled a chair from behind the counter.

John sat down, and Mr. Dozbaba hoisted himself up on the counter. Anna Dozbaba dropped heavily on a shell case close by, and ran her hand through her graying hair to the little knot at the back of her head. A few strands had escaped the severe lines and hung down over her ear.

"We got three boys and one girl, Parson," the storekeeper explained. "Here they are growing up, where decent folks don't even be able to go on the streets at night. For Mamma and me, it don't matter so much. But the children. In a place like this, what becomes of the children? That is what we keep asking each other."

Anna nodded her head in solemn agreement.

John didn't know what to say to them. He couldn't tell them of the heaviness in his heart. He couldn't tell them of his own inadequacy to meet the situation. Seeing the hope in their eyes was like sitting on the bank of a swift river, watching a drowning man, and being unable to swim.

"I'll try my best," he said dubiously.

"To your church we don't belong, Parson," Anna ventured, as though she were afraid that it made a difference. "We are Lutheran."

"But we thought this way, Mamma and I," the storekeeper put in eagerly, "If your church we can help get started, and besides, make our town decent, maybe other peoples will come and other churches will come. When we have a church of our own, then we can think about going to it. Ain't that right, Parson?"

"That's exactly right, Brother Dozbaba. I'd like to have you folks come. It's going to be a tol'able hard job, and we're going to need all the help we can get."

"A place to hold meetings you will need, someone what knows where folks live, to tell you, and a team and buggy to get around with. The store, Mamma can run. I'll go with you."

"There's the Evans, the Millers, the Vaps over on the creek, and ——" Mamma stopped counting with her fingers and straightened up. "There is the ranch peoples and the squatters. What to do, Papa?"

"That's right, they can't never be mixed," Mr. Dozbaba agreed. "Groceries the ranchers won't even buy at the same stores, whiskey at the same saloons they won't drink, or even water their horses at the same troughs with the homesteader's."

This was something that John hadn't planned on. It would make things doubly difficult. "But we can't have the church taking sides in a thing like that. If we're going to get a thing done we're going to have to have the help of both sides. We got to get them together, somehow."

"Not so long while Hart is here. The biggest saloon and the biggest ranch he owns," the storekeeper told him. "And he's got two boys just like him, regular hellions."

"Maybe we can talk to him."

" 'Twon't do no good, I can tell you that."

"With folks fighting that-away, how do you do business here?"

"Well, I tell you," he said, his eyes twinkling. "During the day ranchers buy from us, and at night the homesteaders drive up to the back door by their wagons and get what they want."

There was a light tap at the back door and Dozbaba got up, excusing himself. "When somethings is important sometimes the squatters comes by the back door in daylight." He opened the door and a pale-faced lad of about sixteen came in.

"Maw wants a box of twenty-two's, Dozy," he said. "There's a skunk been gettin' our chickens."

"Till after dark you shouldn't have come, Tommy boy. You make troubles for us, maybe."

"I ain't scared." He laid down the money and swaggered out the back door.

"Out on a homestead that boy lives with his mamma by themselves. His papa was last year killed by a horse. They are trying to farm, and from the Box Bar Y the boys has been pestering the life out of them poor folks."

"It's a sin and shame, Brother Dozbaba. Maybe we can be the means of making peace between them." John got to his feet.

"Maybe. And the sun comes up in the west tomorrow, maybe also. Goodby, Parson. When you are ready to make the calls just come over."

At noon Belle introduced him to the others. There was a girl that he'd never seen before, and half a dozen rough-looking men sitting around the table. Conversation ceased when he came in, and they all looked at him with poorly veiled disgust.

"Got a sermon for us, Parson?" Clara asked, bitterly sarcastic.

"I reckon I could give you a sermon," he replied evenly. "And I don't think it'd go amiss."

Belle thrust her head through the kitchen door and yelled, "Don't you start none of that, Parson, or I'll make you eat out in the barn." They laughed.

Belle brought in a huge bowl of fried potatoes. That was the signal for everyone to begin. They dove for the meat, and gravy, and beans, scooping their plates full.

"If you don't mind," John suggested, "I'd like to ask a blessing."

A burly mule skinner looked up from the task of cutting his meat, and blurted. "Go right ahead, Parson. Go right ahead. Don't let us bother you!"

Belle glared at John, but he bowed his head. The boarders stopped eating and stared at him in amazement as he began, "Bless this food for its intended use. Watch over those of us gathered together for this noon meal. Be with us and guide us and care for us. In Jesus' name we ask Thee, Amen."

Belle was the first to speak when he finished. "Parson," she said, "don't *ever* do that again at my table!"

"I'm sorry you feel that way, Sister Williams," he answered, "But I'm going to ask a blessing anyhow."

Chapter 3

THE next week was a busy one for John. He had a hard time finding a suitable building in which to hold services. The school house wouldn't do at all. It was an abandoned sod shanty that was crowded when a handful of pupils and the teacher packed into it. There was no town hall in Regina Springs. Since Julius Hart, the saloon owner, was the mayor, and his henchmen made up the council, they transacted whatever business was necessary at a table in one corner of the Gold Eagle Saloon. Regularly the elections were held in the same place. John talked to a real estate agent on Main street, but the fellow said bluntly that there weren't any buildings available, and walked away.

"There's a place over by the bank building," Dozbaba said, when John explained his difficulties. "She's not so much to look by, but she might be all right for awhile."

Together they went to a ramshackle old building just off main street. It was a long, narrow structure that seemed about to collapse from age and weathering. The grayish, paintless siding was warped and split, and the front steps were broken on one side, and had been propped up with a couple of bricks.

Inside, it was worse. Great patches of plaster had dropped from the walls and ceiling, exposing the lath, and the place was littered with broken bottles and boxes and plaster. Most of the window panes had long since given way to water-soaked rectangles of cardboard. The floors were wide pine

boards that creaked when one stepped on them, like a pair
of tight shoes; and the dust-laden wind whistled through
the cracks and up around one's ankles. Nevertheless, it was
a building, and the only one that he could locate.

John rented it for five dollars a month, and set to work.
He patched up the plastering as best he could, and talked
the landlord into buying new glass for the windows. He
made the platform and pulpit from odds and ends of lumber that was left over when Dozbaba built his store building, and the seats from ten-inch planks supported by nail
kegs. After a little persuading, the postmaster's wife loaned
her piano, offering her own services as pianist. At last the
building was ready, and John could turn to the task of
organizing.

He and the storekeeper began making the rounds, visit-
ing ranches and homesteads alike. The attitude of the towns-
folk was reflected in the country. A few received them
warmly, but most were decidedly antagonistic towards the
church.

Craig, part owner of the Box Bar Y, was plain spoken.
"There's not going to be no church in Regina Springs," he
raged. "Them blasted nesters come in hanging on the shirt
tails of you preachers. If I was to have my way about it
we'd round up you and all your kind, and ride you out of
town on a rail!"

With that he turned and stalked back into the ranch
house, not giving John the chance to reply. Slowly he and
the Bohemian drove out of the yard towards town. They
went a mile or two without speaking, then Dozbaba said,
"If we could cut a mile across the hills, we'd be up to the
Widow Morelin's place, almost."

John looked over the trackless prairie. "Can we find our way without ary a road to follow?"

"And why not? These hills I know like I know mine own wife, maybe." He turned out across the hills. "Don't feel so bad about that Craig fellow, Parson. He and Hart are partners by the Box Bar Y, and just alike they are. I wouldn't pay no attention —"

A young rider appeared over the hill in front of them. He was a handsome fellow in blue denim dungarees and a wool shirt that was open at the throat. His clean shaven face was hard as the wind and sun that bit into it, and his battered Stetson was yanked down to shade his eyes. He threw one leg over the saddle horn and stared at them.

"Just where are you guys going?" he asked pleasantly.

"Just for the ride we are out, Jimmy."

John looked at his companion in amazement. "As a matter of fact," he said, "we're going over to call on Mrs. Morelin and her son. I'm the new minister at Regina Springs."

The rider flung his foot back into the stirrup and leaned forward. John noted the gun that swung in a worn leather holster at his thigh. "Get back on that trail, Parson, and keep right on going till you get clean off our land. And don't let me catch you back here again! That goes for you too, Dozy!"

"B-b-but Jimmy!" the old storekeeper spluttered. "We didn't mean nothing."

"You heard me," he snapped.

"We don't have to leave," John retorted. "I reckon we'll go right where we're headed."

"Now, Parson, enough troubles we got already, without no more. To get mad with a Hart is one thing, arguments to have with them is a horse of a different smell." Dozbaba turned the team and headed at a fast gait back towards the main trail.

"Better take Dozy's advice, Parson," Jim Hart called after them. "If you want to stay healthy."

"You should have let me talk with him," the Bohemian scolded when they were out of ear shot. "Jimmy is sometimes a bad boy, like his papa he explosions like a firecracker. Already he's foreman of this ranch and the youngest hand on the job is him. It takes a tough one to ride herd on that bunch of men."

"This here's free range," John said angrily. "He hadn't ary right to order us around like a pair of slaves."

"That might be, Parson, but to argue with, he's not the kind of a man, either."

They went out to the road and skirted the Box Bar Y on the way to the Morelin homestead. The widow and Tom were both at the house. She was a spare, gangling, middle-aged woman. Her face was lined with grief, and her eyes looked desperately tired. She offered John a limp hand.

"Howdy do," she said tonelessly. "Won't you come in and set awhile?"

"A church we are going to start in Regina Springs, Mrs. Morelin," Dozbaba announced happily. "You and Tom, we thought maybe, would like to come."

"And why could I come to church?" She sat down in a rocking chair and folded her hands. Her eyes became watery. "What's God ever done for me? My husband Matt brought me and Tom clean out here from Illinois, and there's been nothing but trouble, nothing but trouble. Before he even proved up the homestead he got hisself killed by a horse, leaving me with all this work on my hands. And now them ranchers is hounding the life out of us. God ain't never done me no good."

"God doesn't promise ary one of us an easy life, Sister Morelin. He don't say He's going to make things nice and pleasant for us because we try to live like He wants us to. Some of the finest Christians are hounded by trouble and poverty all their lives. But He does promise to give comfort and help in time of trouble. When things go the worst against us, I reckon that's when we ought to cling the closest to God."

"All my life's ever been is trouble," she wailed. "I never had nothing but trouble, and it looks like that's all I'll have till I go to my grave. How me and Tom'll live this winter is more'n I know."

John talked eagerly, striving to make her see the importance of accepting Christ, but she was immovable in her worry and grief. She rocked to and fro, and wrung her calloused hands while he talked. The tears of self pity gushed, unheeded, down familiar courses in her cheeks. Tom stood beside her, his pinched face as expressionless as the hills in which he lived. His mother's tears hadn't the slightest effect, and John thought that he read a trace of contempt in the boy's eyes.

"Me and Maw'll get along," he boasted confidently. "And one of these days I'll fix them blasted cowpokes that's always nosing around here."

The visitors left the little homestead after getting a reluctant promise from Mrs. Morelin that she and Tom would come to church on Friday evening.

"So heavy with worry is she that she's got no thought of God."

"If we could only make her see what a wonderful source of help He is," John mused. "And show her what this God-lessness will do to her son."

"Ja, ja, but you will find this country is full with peoples like Mrs. Morelin. They're good folks, but their own pleasures, their own problems is so close with their minds that they got no room for Him."

Back at the boarding house John found conditions no better than before. They still poked fun at him when he bowed his head in silent prayer before eating. He tried to talk with several of them, but it was no use. They looked at him blankly, unable to grasp what he was saying. It was as though he spoke an entirely different language.

Only Clara seemed interested. On two occasions he sought her out, and she listened respectfully until he finished. Once or twice she asked a question, and it seemed that the outer shell of hardness was being softened just a little. When he came into the room she spoke to him, and at the table, waited until he raised his head, before starting to eat. However, that could have been because she was sorry for him.

On Friday evening she called him into the parlor, away from the others. "Sit down a minute, Parson. I want to talk to you." She dropped heavily onto the horsehair sofa and began to fan herself with a folded newspaper. Perspiration oozed out of the pores and etched crooked little paths in the powder that clung to her face like dust on a mirror.

He sat on a straight chair opposite her. "What is it you aimed to talk to me about?" he asked hopefully.

"Parson," she snapped, and her fat jowls quivered, "you are not wanted around here. Why don't you pull stakes?"

"I might not be wanted, Sister Williams, because there aren't many of us who like to admit our sins and give up the old way of life. But I am needed here. That's why I got to stay."

"I was talking to Hart today, and he don't like it none that you're barging in here. He figures as how maybe you'll be bad for business."

"I reckon nothing would make me happier," John replied. "I'd as soon tell him as to tell you that if I do get a church going here, my next job'll be to close every saloon in town, and every gambling den like this, too."

"You don't follow me, Parson." She leaned forward and lowered her voice. "You're a nice kid, and I like you. That's why I'm going to all this trouble. Hart's got Regina Springs right under his thumb — like that. And most every man in town jumps when he whistles. He's not easy to buck when he's got his dander up."

"I don't like trouble, Sister Williams, any more'n you do. But I didn't start preaching the Word of God because I thought that it was something easy. If Hart, or anyone else, stands in the way of our getting a church here, we'll have to defeat him, God willing."

She got up and flounced out of the room, her perfume reeking in his nostrils. "Don't say I didn't warn you," she called over her shoulder.

He was well pleased with the crowd that came to the first service. Dozbaba and his wife and children were there, along with Mrs. Morelin and Tom, and quite a few others.

The ranchers stomped boldly inside, spur rowels and chains clanking on the rough pine floors, and guns swinging at their hips. They sat on one side of the improvised church; while the nesters, coming in timidly, sat across the aisle. It was as though some invisible barrier ran through the center of the building, and neither group could cross to the other side.

But they all seemed to get something from the sermon, and at the door after the meeting they were enthusiastic about organizing a church. After everyone had filed out two of the town's leading citizens turned back to speak to him.

"Parson Woodring," one of them began importantly, adjusting his pince nez glasses atop the bridge of his Roman nose. "My name's William Cressland, and this is Arthur O'Connel."

"I'm right glad to know you men," John thrust his hand warmly into theirs.

"We enjoyed your talk tonight."

"Yes sir," O'Connel added. "We sure did."

"I'm happy to hear it. We've got a job to do here in Regina Springs, and it's going to take every one of us to put it over."

"That's what we wanted to talk to you about." Cressland sat down on one end of a plank, and the others followed suit. "You know, Parson, this here town's a tough one."

John smiled. "I reckon I already found that out."

"We thought you would. I told Arthur tonight that I'd bet you already knew it."

"Yeh," O'Connel echoed. "Bill here, said you'd be finding out what kind of a house you're staying in. That's what we came to talk to you about."

John watched them, speculatively, but didn't say anything. Cressland coughed and cleared his throat. "We know that you're a stranger here, and because of that we've decided to overlook it. But you do know, now, what kind of a place you're staying in, don't you?"

"Why yes," he said frankly. "I believe I do."

"Them women, Belle and Clara, are the toughest women in town."

O'Connel smirked approvingly.

John got to his feet and leaned against the pulpit. He saw what was coming, and it angered him. "I've gathered as much."

"Then you are going to move?"

"No, gentlemen, I'm not." He stood erect. "Like you say, that place is a den of evil. I want it cleaned out as bad as you do, but I reckon those souls is as important to God as yours and mine. I want to help them if I can."

"But you can help from the outside, without stirring up all this talk. Everybody in town is shocked to think you're living at that gambling house."

"Yes, we're upright, moral citizens, and we want a Parson what we can look up to. We don't want one we've got to keep apologizin' for."

"I hope you never have to apologize for me." The corners of his mouth began to twitch. "Living at the boarding house isn't going to hurt me. If I move I'll lose the day to day contact with them that I need so much. I honestly feel called to stay; for a while at least, until I see for certain whether some one of them might be brought to Christ."

"You can't do nothing with people like that, Parson. We think you had ought to leave them alone."

"I've got very good authority for it." His hand gripped the Bible he held, a little tighter. "When the Pharisees criticised Christ for eating with a Publican, He told them that those who were well had no need of a physician. Them folks at the boarding house, or gambling house, which ever you choose to call it, are sick morally and spiritually. I reckon I've got to help them if I can."

"But you can't do that kind of people no good," Cressland countered sharply.

"We've decided that we're not going to bring our families to your meetings until you come to your senses. If you don't have no respect for the church, we have."

Then the red hair got the better of him, and his temper flared. "I'm sorry, gentlemen. I'd counted on your help in building a church here, but my duty lies with folks like Belle and Clara fully as much as it does with you. If you want to attend our services in the future, you'll be heartily welcome. Good night."

They flounced out of the door like a pair of bantam roosters with their tail feathers singed. John blew out the lights and locked the building carefully. Almost as soon as his anger flared, it had simmered away, but the damage was done. Was he right in staying at the gambling house? Or should he move? Was he desecrating God, as they inferred, by subjecting himself, and his occupation to ridicule? He had been so positive that he was right only a moment or two before, but now, doubt welled high within him.

The Bishop had warned him to control his temper and his tongue, but on his first attempt he had disregarded the warning and ruined whatever chances there were of getting a church soon. Those men, who carried weight and influence with the better element in Regina Springs, were through with him. They wouldn't trust him, or help now, even tho he were to move. And it was his fault, just as surely as though he had closed the door to them.

As he walked home in the hot night air he wished that
Martha were with him. Since he had known her he had
looked to her for advice. She would know what he should
do; whether he should remain at the boarding house or
move, whether to apologize to the two men who had sought
him out, or whether to quit altogether and go back to
the farm in Missouri. But more than her advice he wanted
someone sympathetic to talk with, who would hold his
hand and listen while he poured out his troubles, and pray
with him for guidance.

He looked up at the stars, pin points of white against
and iridescent blanket of blue that pressed close about him,
until it seemed that he had only to lift his hand to pluck
a star from the heavens. The moon was a crescent shaped
sliver of gold that hung just above the tree tops. Martha
loved nights like this; and, though one could only see a little
patch of the sky for the Ozark trees, they had lain on their
backs for hours, marvelling at the magnitude of the universe,
and at its beauty. This night would have touched a flame
to her eyes, and left them glowing.

John went upstairs and wrote Martha a long letter,
telling her of all the problems that he was up against, of
his own dejection and uncertainity. Somehow he felt better
after that.

Chapter 4

JULIUS Hart was sitting with the Williams sisters in the parlor of the boarding house after supper Saturday evening. Parson John was up in his room going over his sermon, and the rest of the boarders were lined abreast of the bars, about town, bent on getting drunk enough, to sleep through Sunday afternoon. The crowd on the other side of the partition was hilarious, and the roistering and lewd voices could be heard all over the house. Dice were clattering on the tables, only to be drowned by the screeching of a fiddle and the scrape of dancing feet.

"That star boarder of yours is sure gettin' in my hair," Hart said.

"Maybe you think he's not gettin' in mine," Belle retorted. "With him bowing his head before he eats my grub, like he was askin' the Lord to keep it from poisoning him. Him with his fine talk, and praying, acting all the time like he's better'n we are."

"Yeh, that gets me too, but what I really don't like is the way he's getting the nesters stirred up. Before the month is out they'll be flocking around him and followin' like a herd of sheep. New ones'll be coming in, and the first thing you know folks like us'll have to move on. We won't be decent enough for them."

"We got to get him out of here, that's all there is to it."

"You and me think alike, Belle," he said. "One of these fine days I'm going to up and marry you."

"Aw, quit your kiddin'." She flushed a little in spite of herself.

"But right now, would you consider helping me on a little deal, for — say fifty iron men per each?"

"For fifty bucks, Julius Hart," she leaned forward and snuffed out her cigarette in the ash tray, "I'd even marry you. What's the deal?" They all laughed at that.

"There's fifty in it for you, too, Clara."

"You can count me out," Clara announced firmly. "I've seen you make fun of him just about all I can stand."

"Don't be like that," Belle said angrily. "A body'd think you were in love with him."

"You know it ain't so," she countered. "I just don't like to see a whole town pick on one guy, that's all."

"You wouldn't want me to have the marshall pick you up on Monday, and slam you into jail, now would you?"

"On what charge?"

He leaned back in the chair and puffed a cloud of acrid cigar smoke ceilingward. "Just suppose you let me worry about the charge."

"You got no call to talk that way, J. C.," Belle snapped, her eyes blazing.

"Oh, ain't I?"

"No. If Clara don't want to she don't have to help. And you, or no one else, is going to make her."

"You're mighty brave for Clara, aren't you, darlin'?" Hart retorted. "I'd bet you wouldn't be spouting off so easy if you was in her shoes. You know I could take care of that, too."

"Just you try threatenin' me, J. C. Hart. Just you try it!" She got up and stepped closer to him.

Clara's gaze had fallen. "There's no call getting huffy, Belle," she said dully. "I'll help. What do you want me to do?"

"Well now, that's better. That's much better. You're going to think this fifty bucks is the easiest money you ever did earn."

* * *

Sunday morning was the beginning of a beautiful summer day. The wind was as cool and soft as a maiden's kiss, and the sun's heat was diffused by large, fleecy thunderheads. It was the kind of a day that seemed to make each man his neighbor's brother. Hate and narrowness vanished.

John went down to the store building early. Cressland's threat that folks weren't coming to church until he moved, disturbed him greatly. Saturday he worked hard, placing his position before all that he could call upon, but no one could tell what was going on in the minds behind those bland, expressionless faces. Whether or not it had been successful, he would soon know.

The night before he spent tossing and rolling, sleeplessly, in his bed. For awhile he would think that he had been right, and that surely the others would see that the only way he could hope to have any effect upon Belle and her crowd was to remain there in the gambling house, until, at least, he was convinced that the task was hopeless. And again he was assailed by doubt. He was risking the whole church on the outside chance that some one, he dare not hope for more, at the house might be drawn close to God. Now the die was cast, and success or failure would be his.

He selected the songs for Sunday School and Church, and distributed the books along the seats; then went over the planks with a dust cloth to remove the film that had collected over night, and evened the shades once more. At nine-thirty he threw open the doors, expecting to find a group of scrubbed and happy youngsters waiting on the steps, as they had done in Hanridge. But there were none. He sat down on the little porch and waited. People passed by, but as they did, they turned their heads and pretended not to notice him. Nine forty-five and ten o'clock came and passed, still no one arrived.

An icicle stabbed through his heart. Cressland had made good his threat, there would be no one at Sunday School or Church. The Dozbaba family, with all their promises of faithfulness, had forsaken him, the same as everyone else. His first thought was to leave town at once. He was licked, finished. His head dropped to his arms. A silent prayer went up from his dejected heart, a prayer for wisdom, and courage, and peace of soul.

How many saw him hunched miserably on the steps, he didn't know. Suddenly he straightened, and pulled out his watch. It was five minutes to eleven. He had announced church at eleven o'clock, and there was going to be church. If anyone did come in they weren't going to find him without a service to offer. Besides, somebody from the country *might* come in. He stalked up to the pulpit.

In a clear, loud voice he announced the first song. "We shall open the morning worship by singing number 323 in the hymnal, 'When the Roll is Called up Yonder'." There was no piano accompaniment, but he began bravely,

"When the trumpet of the Lord shall sound
And time shall be no more,
And the morning breaks eternal bright and fair . . ."

His unmelodious baritone rang through the small building on the chorus.

"When the roll is called up yonder,
When the roll is called up yonder,
When the roll is called up yonder,
When the roll is called up yonder,
I'll be there."

It must have sounded odd to anyone going past, and it would have seemed doubly odd had they stopped and looked in at the door.

He was on the second verse when there was a faint sound on the steps outside, and two women came in. He was astonished, for it was Belle and Clara Williams. They were heavily rouged, and dressed in shiny black satin that rustled when they walked, like a wind through parched corn stalks. Their arms and necks were weighted with cheap jewelry, and Clara's hat was graced with a white ostrich plume that arched over her left ear. They stopped in the doorway, and stared at the empty seats, the empty choir row, and at John who was singing fervently as he walked towards them.

They would have left, but he took Belle by the arm, handed Clara his open book; and, still smiling, showed them to their seats, well up in front. He knew the hymn by heart, and continued to sing while he found the page in another book.

"We'll all sing the last verse," he announced, lifting his hands. They stood up. Reluctantly, two brittle, off key sopranos joined his own flat baritone on the last verse.

"Let us labor for the Master from dawn till setting sun
  Let us talk of all His wondrous love and care . . ."

It was probably the strangest church service that was held anywhere that day. The two women were squirming uncomfortably, as though they didn't want to stay, but couldn't quite bring themselves to walking out. John went through the entire service as though the room were filled. He made all the announcements for the coming week, sang a hymn for a solo, and passed the collection plate himself. He couldn't help but notice that Clara dropped in a dollar bill, while Belle put in a few pennies and a dime that she happened to have in her purse.

He preached more than just a sermon. He forgot the text and the prepared talk that had been so carefully rehearsed, and was lying on the pulpit beside him. Folding his hands, he leaned forward and pleaded earnestly with them. His voice was soft and firm, and his eyes never wavered from theirs, as he insisted again and again that they must accept Christ as their Personal Saviour.

He painted beautiful word pictures, pictures of their own degrading sin, contrasted with the wondrous glory of God, and of Christ hanging on the Cross for them — that was a picture that they had never seen before.

He thought that he was making an impression upon Clara, for her gaze fell, and she dabbed at her eyes with the corner of her handkerchief. But Belle sat there, as stoic as though she were carved from stone.

He was pleading for them, and something more. He was pleading for the chance to remain in Regina Springs, and to have another try at establishing a permanent church. He was pleading for those youngsters who feared to go out on the streets; for their mothers who would watch tearfully as they grew older and went the errant, uncaring way of the community.

Finally it was over. John waited in the pulpit, praying that they might come forward to learn more of the Word of God. But they bustled out of the seats and fairly skimmed up the aisle in their haste. He stared after them sorrowfully.

Carefully he gathered up the song books and piled them beside the door, where he would put them back in the box the following day. He had scrimped to buy those books. They were to have helped him put a church in the wildest little town east of Cheyenne. Well, the wild little town had beaten him, just as everyone said that it would. He was going back to the Ozarks to his father's farm, where he belonged. He wasn't meant to be a preacher, anyway. He suspected that before, but now he was sure. He must have been mistaken in thinking that he was called to the ministry. Martha would be disappointed at first, and so would his parents, but they would get over it.

Back at his room he found a letter that had been shoved under the door. They must have forgotten to give it to him the day before. It was from Martha, and had been written before she received his last letter. It exuded confidence and hope and faith, and asked a hundred questions about his work. He crumpled it and threw it in the waste basket. Then sat down and wrote a short note to Bishop King, resigning his post and telling of his decision to quit the ministry.

As he started out the boarding house door to mail it, Belle came from the parlor and laid her hand on his arm.

"I'd like to talk to you, Parson." Her voice was taut with emotion, but he couldn't be sure whether it was anger, or something else.

He felt little like talking to anyone at the moment, but because her manner was so insistent he followed her into the parlor and sat down. It was the first time that she had ever deliberately spoken to him.

"I suppose you're wondering why Clara and me came to church this morning," she began.

"I reckon I have wondered about that." His own voice carried an irritating edge. "But I was glad to see you there, no matter what fetched you."

"Well, it wasn't to do you no good," she replied bluntly. "Julius Hart was over last night. He gave me and Clara fifty bucks apiece to go down there today, and break up the meeting." If she expected a reaction she was disappointed because his expression didn't change. "Then *his* marshall was going to give you a ninety days suspended sentence that you'd have to serve if you ever come back to town."

"I see." He had to fight to control himself. "Maybe it's a good thing that nobody but you two came to church today. There's just one question that I'd like to ask you. Why are you telling me all this?"

"Because," her eyes were downcast, and she twisted her handkerchief into a tight little knot. "I'm telling you because I feel so low and cheap, like a bully kicking a fellow when he's down."

John smiled wanly. "I guess being 'down' describes me all right," he said. "The decent people won't come to

church, and the rest of the town is schemin' to chase me
out. A fellow couldn't be 'down' much lower than I am."

"It's my fault, isn't it? About the decent people, I mean."

He looked at her queerly. It wasn't like Belle to be con-
cerned about the trouble she might have caused him. "I'd
rather not say."

"It's because you're living here, I know that. We used
to think it was quite a joke, you staying on when folks
was talking about you like they was. I'm awful sorry, truly
I am."

"Thank you, Sister Williams," his voice choked. "That's
the kindest words I've heard since I've been in Regina
Springs."

There was a long, painful silence, then she blurted suddenly, "That preachin' of yours cut clean through me.
Some of them things I haven't heard since Maw used to
read to us kids before we went to bed. I haven't got no right
to ask, Parson, not none at all. But would Christ, could
He take a wicked woman like me?" Her voice quavered.

"He took Mary Magdalene," John said simply. " *'Him
that cometh unto me, I will in no wise cast out,'* Christ
told us. It don't matter what you've been, or what you've
done. When you give your heart to Him the past is wiped
out in one fell stroke. There isn't any difference among
any of us before we accept Christ, we all have sinned so
much, and come so far short of the Glory of God."

For the next few minutes he told her the story of Mary
Magdalene, because her life quite closely paralleled Belle's
own. He told her of Mary's scarlet life of sin, how she
accepted the Master, and by her magnificent character and
love, made herself beloved of Him. Belle's eyes softened
as he talked, and the lines in her face lost their harshness.

"The important thing first, is to give your heart and soul, completely to Him."

"Parson," she said softly, "I want to be a Christian more than anything else in the world."

"You realize what it is to be a Christian, don't you, Sister Williams? All this," he swept the room with his hand, "All this'll have to be put aside."

"How do I go about it?" she persisted. "What do I do to become a Christian?"

He took his Bible and quickly thumbed the pages to John 1:12. "The first thing is to go to God's Own Word for guidance," he said. " *'But as many as received Him, to them gave He power to become sons of God, even to them that believe on His name'.*"

"Can I see it?" she asked hoarsely. "I've never read the Bible very much." She went over the verse slowly to herself, pronouncing each word with her lips.

"Now read Acts 16:31 and Ephesians 2:8-9."

Belle fumbled through the well worn Bible, without the faintest idea of where to find the verses he suggested. Without commenting, John leaned forward and turned to the sixteenth chapter of Acts. When she concluded that bit of Scripture he found the place in Ephesians.

"Do you see what is necessary to become a Christian?" he asked.

"To take Jesus into my heart and tell Him how much I've sinned against Him," she stammered, "—and tell Him how I can't live any more without Him?"

"That's right, Belle. That's the beginning of all Christianity. It don't matter whether we're rich or poor, moral or immoral, when we come to Christ we've all got to come through the door of faith."

"But I do believe in Him, Parson."

"Let us pray," he said, kneeling. She got to her knees beside him. To her, it seemed the most logical thing to do. "Now pray, *'God, be merciful to me, a sinner'*." She repeated the words after him. There, on the parlor floor, she gave herself to Christ, and when at last she raised her head, her eyes were radiant. A smile shown through the tears, and for the first time in her life she was completely happy.

Later he told her of the sacrifices that she would be called upon to make, and the abuse that would be heaped upon her. "You'll find that it won't be easy to be a Christian," he concluded. "These so called good people won't accept you for a long time, if ever. And Hart, your boarders, and most of your friends will never rest until they've tried every possible way to shake you from Christ."

"I hope that I'll remain true."

"The secret of keeping your faith fresh and strong lies in this Book, Sister Williams. Go to it daily, and then through it the Holy Spirit will lead you closer to Him. And when you've read it, pray to the Father. It's only by walking and talking with God *every day* that He can show you His will and His love.

"And don't forget that 'If any man be in Christ, he is a new creature': your life will be filled with the love of Christ, which passes knowledge!"

"Where would I start to read the Bible?" she asked timidly.

"You might start with Romans 10:9-10, Psalms 107, and I Corinthians 10-13. Here, I'll write them down."

"Thanks, Parson."

"They'll give you some idea of what a Christian should be."

The letter to Bishop King lay, forgotten, in his pocket.

It was Clara who couldn't sleep that night. She went to bed at the regular time, but her mind wouldn't let her rest. Every time she closed her eyes she saw the Parson pointing his finger accusingly at her, while his mild brown eyes probed to the depths of her soul.

Was there a God, or wasn't there? Before, she had never bothered much about God, only hearing His name in blasphemy. But now she couldn't force thoughts of Him from her mind. It had to be decided, once and for all.

She reached out and touched the cold, iron bedstead. It was forty years old, and had been her mother's before her. In another forty years, after she was gone, that bedstead would still be just the same. Life was moving and unstable, more fragile, even, than the material things that one used so casually. Was that all there was to living? It was the principle that her life had been based upon. She'd been living for the moment, squeezing it dry of every drop of excitement and gaiety; not daring to think of the morrow. But was that the way to live? Did life just mean for one to be born, and live a span, and die? Was there nothing more to it than that? She got up and sat for a long time on the side of her bed.

She felt strangled, and all the breath gone out of her, as if some one had wounded her terribly. "O God — God!" she said intensely over and over, hanging on to that thin ray of Light for dear life. It was so faint that she could hardly see it at all. "But I'll try so hard, Father, to find you! I'll read the Word, and I'll come to You often for help — I need You so much!"

Chapter 5

At the supper table that evening John bowed his head in silent prayer, just as he always did.

"What's the matter, Parson? Are you sick?" A rough section hand bawled from the far end of the big table. "You just got a hangover, that's all. A good drink of whisky'll fix you up dandy."

"That's what I always use," another put in. "Here, I got some I can let you have. Just a minute, and I'll get a shot for you." He leaned forward, groping around on the floor for his bottle.

"Shut up, you crazy galoot. You're botherin' the Parson so he can't hardly hear his self talk to his self."

John began to eat, as though he didn't hear what they said. Belle watched him, then gritted her teeth and bowed her head in a similar blessing.

"Now what's wrong with you, Belle?" Pete Langford demanded gruffly.

"She does look sort of pale."

The heavy lipstick was gone from her face, and her frowzled, peroxide bleached hair had been pulled close to her head and pinned. John watched her closely for some clue as to how her newly found faith would weather its first test. Her mouth was set resolutely, and her eyes shone.

"Are you sick too. Belle?"

"Maybe she and the Parson were out on a spree last night."

When the laughter died Pete said, "Maybe she's got religion, too."

"That's right, Pete," she replied evenly. Exploding a bomb in the dining room would have caused no more excitement than that announcement did. He dropped his fork and stared at her in open mouthed amazement. General conversation choked off, short. "You all know what I've been in the past. I've gambled and drank, and done about everything in the book. Now I want to say that all of those things are behind me. I am a Christian, and I'm proud to be able to say it."

"What kind of a joke is this?" Langford asked incredulously.

She shook her head proudly. "It isn't a joke, Pete. I never was so serious about anything in my life. I only wish that the rest of you could come to believe in Christ, too. I'm just starting to live."

At that moment John knew that he had laid the foundation well, and that, no matter how much outside pressure was exerted upon her, she would never be turned from the Master. He thanked God for the courage that He had given her.

"I never thought you'd go soft on us, Belle," one of the men exclaimed.

"What's Hart going to think of this? I'll bet he'll take this here religious stuff out of you."

"You'd lose your money, fellow," she retorted sharply.

"I suppose that the next thing you'll want to do is to close the other half of the house," Pete said sarcastically. "You'll be too high falutin' to live on gambling money."

"You've called the trick, Pete. The roulette wheels, faro tables, and the whole works go out tomorrow, including the bar."

"Then we'll move!" He cursed violently.

"Oh, no you won't," Clara announced. "I got something to say around here. Them tables stay, and the bar stays. Whether Belle sticks or not don't make no difference to me."

"I'd like to talk to you a few minutes, Clara," she said softly.

"All right, but don't think you're getting away with anything."

When the women had gone upstairs to their room the boarders turned on John vehemently. "This is some of your work, Parson," they accused.

"It is, but I'm not ashamed of it. I reckon I'm mighty proud of Belle right now, for the way she's letting Christ into her life."

"Hart'll let something into you, all right," Pete growled, "whenever he hears about this. He most owns this joint and I'm bettin' he ain't going to let you and Belle pull no deal like this."

"We should've knowed better than to let a nosey Sky Pilot stick around here. I told Hart something like this'd happen."

Two or three of the more belligerent got out of their chairs and took a step towards John.

"We'd ought to run you out of town, tonight," they blustered. "Before you do any more damage!"

John's knuckles began to itch, just as they had when he was a boy, fighting three times a week to keep his reputation intact.

"You men are afraid of me, and afraid of the Gospel I preach," he told them, without raising his voice. "If you weren't you wouldn't be so mad at me. As for the damage you're talking about, I'm going to do all that kind of damage I can. So, I reckon if there's anything you want to do about it, you'd better start right now."

"You won't talk so big if we do pitch in to you." They grumbled and threatened, but soon scattered to the saloons or the gambling tables on the other side of the house. The tinny, off key clatter of the old piano, and shuffle of dancing feet, floated through the thin partition.

Upstairs, Belle was pleading desperately with her sister. "We've never been very close to each other," she said. "It's prob'ly my fault as much as it is yours. But now, Clara, I want you to find the same happiness I've found."

"Hmph," Clara snorted derisively. "I'd trade my share of it for three fingers of rye, right now."

"I know how you feel. I hadn't even thought about God since Maw used to tell us about Him when we were kids. You remember, she read her Bible every night."

"Yeh, and what did it ever do for her? She lost everything Paw left her and us, except this old barn we're livin' in, and she died a pauper. The same thing'd happen to us if we closed things downstairs."

Belle found herself strangely inarticulate. There were so many things that she wanted to say to Clara, about Christ taking care of them, and having faith. The Parson had made it all sound so beautiful, and it was that way in her own heart; but the words seemed to be piling up like logs above a dam, just behind her tongue.

"I wish you'd give it a try, Clara. Just for a month. We'll take out the tables downstairs and close the bar, even if we do lose the boys as boarders by doin' it. During the month we'll read the Bible every night and pray that He'll take care of us, and come into your heart like He's come into mine."

"Nothing doing," Clara lashed. "You've made both of us the laughing stock of the town. You'll not get me into no such crazy scheme as that to finish the job."

There were tears in the older woman's eyes, "Isn't there anything I can say that'll make you change your mind?" she asked.

"You know there ain't. And don't talk to me about throwing out the gambling tables again. The house is in my name, and there's nothing you can do about it."

"I suppose you're right," Belle answered. "I can't make you throw them out, but I can quit living off the money that's made there."

"It's all right with me if you want to be a fool."

"I'll take care of the boarders, and I'll live on half of what comes in from it."

Hart was over to see Belle as soon as word got to him that evening. He wouldn't believe that it was true until she told him about it herself.

"You'll be over this in a day or two," he assured her confidently. "You just got in there and let that blasted Parson cut loose a lot of hell and high water preachin' and it kind of got under your skin. In a little while you'll be ashamed of the fool you're making of yourself. This ain't nothing but a passing fancy. Come on, Belle, why don't you be sensible?"

"I am being sensible, Julius. I've never been more sensible in my life."

Then he lost his temper. "What I told Clara about being picked up by the marshall can happen to you, too."

"You had ought to know by now that bluffing never did work with me, Julius Hart. Even if you did put me in jail you couldn't change me back to the way you want me. All I can say is, do your worst."

He stormed out of the house.

John was jubilant over Belle's sudden reversal of character. It was worth all the difficulty that his staying at the Williams' place had caused, just to see the light in her eyes. Anyone looking at her could tell that Christ had come into her life. She was a gnarled oak tree suddenly bursting into full leaf, after standing, barren and ugly, throughout a bleak winter. Her step was light, and her harsh, lined face was gentle and kind. Even her strident voice softened. Now that she had been converted, John was sure that the criticism against him would gradually disappear, and folks would begin to understand his point of view.

Belle soon found that he was right about the good people of Regina Springs. Men who used to slip over to the Williams house regularly for a riotous night of drinking and gambling, disliked speaking to her in respectable society, and their wives refused to accept her as an equal. At prayer meetings, the few who came sat apart from her, and spoke reservedly. They didn't wish to snub her openly, and yet were unwilling to treat her as a friend. John marvelled at Belle's courage. She smiled at every rebuff, and

went out of her way to be kind to those who were the
meanest to her.

Things were much more difficult for Belle at home than
she ever imagined that they could be. When the boarders
discovered that she was in earnest they left her strictly
alone, speaking to her only when it was absolutely necessary. And then their voices were heavy with sarcasm. When
she entered the room where they were talking, conversation lagged to long, embarrassing silences. Only when
she left was it renewed. Every week they paid their board
bills, making it quite plain that they stayed on solely on
account of Clara.

But it didn't seem to bother Belle at all. Her faith blos-
somed under John's tutelage, and her Bible was used more
in a day than it had been used in the past fifteen years.
She continued to pray fervently every night that Clara
might yield to the Master. Though she couldn't get her
sister to listen to her at all, she urged John to try talking
with her.

At Belle's insistence he did so, but she remained aloof.
He had never talked with anyone so strange. Clara listened
in silence, clinging to every word as though she was moved
by his persuasion. Her questions were apt and intelligent,
showing that she was thinking. It seemed that she was
hanging in the balances, now leaning this way, and again
that; waiting for him to quote the right bit of scripture,
or say the right word to win her for Christ. Her attitude
bothered him greatly, and he added his prayers to those of
Belle.

There were so many things that could be holding Clara
to her sinful life. It could be the attitude of her friends,
the pressure Hart brought to bear, or it could be the love

of wealth. He had watched her face, as she came from the gambling den, after some luckless rancher had lost a ship-ment of beef over one of the tables, and the lust that lurked in her eyes wasn't a pleasant thing to see.

Towards the end of the week an incident happened that greatly annoyed John. He had been out for a long walk in the evening, and was just returning to the house when Clara met him on the porch. He thought it strange because she was very obviously dressed for the occasion. Her fat arms protruded from the black satin sleeves of the same bizarre outfit that she had worn to church. Her hair had been freshly peroxided and fuzzed with a curling iron. It was tied with a wide ribbon of brilliant red. The place reeked with a nauseating perfume.

"It's a nice evening, isn't it, Parson?" she proffered, in a tone that she had never used before in speaking to him.

"Yes, isn't it?"

He paused a moment, and she sidled close to him.

"I'd like to have a few minutes to talk to you, if you don't mind?"

Perhaps this was it. Perhaps their prayers and urging had had a telling effect, and she, too, was ready to give herself to Christ. "Of course, Sister Williams,' he agreed. "I'm happy for the chance to talk to you."

They went into the parlor, and he sat down on one end of the horsehair sofa.

"Where's Belle?"

"How should I know?" Clara snapped, sitting down beside him. "I suppose she went upstairs to bed." For the space of two or three minutes they sat and looked at each other. "Parson," she said, so abruptly that she startled him. "What's the matter with me?"

He looked at her in amazement.

"You're the only fellow I ever met that didn't like me, even a little bit."

"Why, I like you, Sister Williams," he said uncomfortably.

"Well, you don't show it very much." She slipped a bit closer to him, and he moved away. He would have suspected that the boarders were pulling this as a joke, if it wasn't for Clara's face. Her eyes reflected the tortures of an aching heart.

"Why, I'd even go for this stuff Belle's so wrapped up in, if you'd just be nice to me once in a while. I'm sure I could be a Christian for *you*." She spoke reluctantly, as though she were an automaton and some irresistible force were drawing out the words, one by one.

Beads of perspiration oozed out around John's collar, and all at once the room became stifling.

"If I understand you rightly, Sister Williams," he said gently, and in as impersonal a tone as he could muster, "and I reckon I do, I'm awfully sorry. You see, I don't have the right to like anyone that-away no more. I'm engaged to be married."

She hung her head shamefacedly. "I'm sorry, Parson. I shouldn't of said nothing, but I just couldn't help it. You won't tell anyone, will you?"

"Of course I won't tell anyone." When she raised her eyes he went on. "I wish that you would follow Belle's example. Your present way of living doesn't satisfy you, does it?"

"I get along."

"Yes, you get along," he said softly. "Just like the boarders who stay here, and the men who gamble their living away at your gaming tables. They live from one day to the next, not caring for anything but the present. Jesus will give your life direction and purpose, Sister Williams. Life'll mean something to you; and you'll know real happiness, the kind that only He can fetch."

"You and Belle preach at me all day!" she blurted, jumping to her feet. "I ain't goin' to listen to any more of it!" she sobbed, and ran from the room.

For an hour or more John sat on the sofa without moving, staring into the darkness beyond the yellow circle of light. What had he done to cause her to become infatuated with him? Had he, by some word or action, led her to believe that he returned her love? That must have been the case, or she'd never have staged the scene just now. Something encouraged her. Sighing, he got to his feet and made his way up to his room.

Chapter 6

FRIDAY of the following week John was sitting at the dinner table when the station agent knocked at the door, and asked for him.

"I got a telegram for you, Parson. It came this mornin', but I didn't get away to deliver it till right now. A fellow can't go traipsing all over town with fifty cent telegrams."

It wasn't often that he received a telegram, and his hand shook a little as he opened it. The station agent stood to one side, with his hands thrust deep in his pockets, and teetered on his heels.

"Meet Friday Afternoon Train," was all that the message said. It was signed, "Martha."

"If there isn't no answer, I'll be gettin' back," the agent reminded him.

He shook his head. "There isn't any answer."

What could it mean? Was she sending him an important package, or could it be — he dare not even think it — but, she might be coming herself! He went upstairs and put on a clean shirt, and straightened out his tie. His trousers needed pressing, but there wasn't time.

As usual the train was late. He paced the platform impatiently; looking up the road-bed to the place where the track blended into the horizon, and going into the stuffy little depot to stare at the clock. He tried talking to the grumpy station agent, but could get no more than a short "yes," or "no" in answer to his questions.

His hat was shoved back on his forehead, revealing a disheveled shock of red hair, and he had pulled at his tie until the knot was barely visible under his coat lapel. He leaned against the corner of the depot and tried to appear nonchalant, but it was no use. Every two minutes he persisted in craning his neck, like a small boy at a circus, trying to spot some sign of the train.

At last there was a forlorn whistle in the distance. His heart faltered in its course, then resumed its pounding in bass drum tempo. The agent sauntered out onto the platform with the orders for the crew, and John followed breathlessly.

The train struggled, and groaned, and lurched into the yard. He ran alongside the lone coach, trying to catch a glimpse of her among the passengers.

She was there, standing on the steps when the train stopped! With a delighted little squeal she ran into his arms, and he kissed her fiercely. He had almost forgotten how pretty she was, with her little, up-turned nose and saucy smile.

"Darling!" He lifted her high, and whirled her about, her long skirts billowing in the wind.

"It's so good to see you, John," she murmured, after regaining her breath. "I been standing in the aisle with my satchel in my hands ever since that old train left North Platte."

"Hey there, Parson," the station agent yelled, "what's Belle goin' to think of that? And right out in broad daylight, too?"

"Belle?" Twin flames kindled in Martha's eyes, and she pulled away. "Who's Belle?"

John reddened, and he stammered guiltily when he tried to explain. "I—I'll tell you all about it on the way uptown. There hasn't never been anything between us, honest there hasn't. Why, she's ten, fifteen years older than me."

Martha accepted his explanation stiffly, as though she didn't quite believe all of it. "I'm plumb forgetting my manners. Nancy, I want you to meet John Woodring. John, this is Nancy Riley. She's my best friend. Her Paw's a singer who's been helping with some revival meetings down our way. When I asked her to come along, I reckoned on staying longer than I'm going to."

He nodded stiffly to Nancy, then turned back to Martha. "Now don't act that-away, honey. I can explain ever'thing."

"I don't doubt that you can."

She started down the wide, board walk, and John grabbed up their suitcases and caught up with her. Nancy tagged along, half a dozen steps behind.

"This is the most forsakenest place I ever did see," she observed, to no one in particular. "I expected a whole passel of trees, and hills, and things like that. Why, these here hills ain't no more'n little piles of sand. You could put the whole lot of them in one medium-sized Ozark mountain, and never find them."

Neither Martha nor John were listening. He was trying to explain about Belle and Clara, and she was walking haughtily at his side.

"You didn't have to be so friendly that folks started talking about it," she said.

"But I wasn't any more friendly with her than I was with the rest of the congregation," he protested. "A body's got to be nice to people."

"It sounds like you been nice to her, very nice, if you ask me."

"I didn't ask you," he snapped.

While they walked half a block neither spoke. Martha cast a sidelong glance at John, and he watched her out of the corner of his eye. At the crossing he stopped and grasped her shoulders, turning her around until she faced him.

"Belle's the only friend I got in Regina Springs," he said. "I already told you how she's trying to be Christian, and how that whole bunch is dead set against her. She's needing my help to keep her faith and courage high, as much as I'm needing yours. Believe me."

Martha took hold of his coat lapels with her tiny, work-roughened hands; hands that had known a man's work in the field, as well as caring for a home.

"I do believe you, John dear," she said. "I reckon I'd believe what you told me, no matter what it was."

He beamed happily.

In front of Dozbaba's store, he paused. He could stand the jeers and scorn of the boarding house himself, and the gossip that had been caused by his living there. But he didn't want Martha and Nancy to be subjected to it. He took them into the general store, and persuaded the genial old Bohemian lady to rent them a room.

After supper he came back to visit with Martha. Mrs. Dozbaba shooed the children into their bedroom, and led her husband out into the kitchen.

"I'll be getting myself out of the way," Nancy said. "You don't want me around here watching and listening to what you got to say."

When she was gone John said softly, "There's a question I've been wanting to ask you, Martha, ever since this afternoon when you came."

"Yes?" Her voice was soft and leading.

"Why did you come here?"

"I reckoned as how you needed me. When you wrote that you didn't have ary a friend, and no one to help you, I just had to come. There's a lot of work to be done here, and together you and I'll get a church going, no matter if the whole country is against us."

"I do need help, darling, and I don't know of anyone as'd be more help than you." He took her hand. "Sometimes I get so discouraged, I don't feel like going on another day."

"You hadn't ought to feel like that," she said. "You got a great work to do here, God's work."

"I reckon you're right, but I can't have you go through all this. I ain't got nothing to offer you as long as I stay here. A Parson don't get much money in a place like this; and besides, you'd be talked about, and laughed at, and hated like they hate me."

"I'd be proud to be hated that way." Her brown eyes flashed.

"You're a wonderful girl, Martha. I don't know what I'd do without you."

"You'd better not try," she chided.

"Would you marry me tomorrow?"

Her lips answered for her as she leaned forward and put her arms about his neck.

And so they decided upon being married the following day. They would have to drive to North Platte for a marriage license, and a minister to perform the ceremony. They invited Nancy to go along, to act as the maid of honor.

Early the next morning John went down to the livery stable to rent a horse and buggy.

"All I got's that there mare." The liveryman pointed a grimy forefinger at an old mare that was drooping sickly in the back stall. Her bony hips were pushing up under her skin, like the poles on a tent, and her ears lopped outward, as though she lacked the strength to hold them erect. Her legs spraddled, one bracing against the other, probably to keep her from falling. In fact, she looked as if she might collapse like the one hoss shay, if someone laid a finger on her.

John looked her over dubiously. "She looks kind of funny. Is she sick?"

"Would I be renting you a sick horse? She's gettin' old, and she ain't so fast as some, maybe; but she's as sound as a dollar. It's either take it or leave it. Makes no difference to me."

"I would like to have a little better horse, but I reckon she'll do." John got out his pocketbook and fished for a couple of bills. "I'm getting married today."

The liveryman spat out a wad of tobacco juice and squinted at him from one good eye. "Hmph," he snorted, unimpressed. "There'll be a fifty buck deposit."

"Fifty dollars?"

"That's right. So's I'll be sure of gettin' my horse and buggy back."

"Oh, I'll return her to you. You can trust me."

"I don't trust no one, especially preachers."

"Well, I—I'll be back in a few minutes with the money."

He had only seventy-five dollars. It was going to cut them awfully short, with a ring to buy, and a minister to pay, but it would have to do. When he got back to the stable the horse was tied to the hitching rack in front. He got in and drove up to the Dozbaba store.

Martha was waiting, a bit frightenedly, just inside the door. John had never seen her looking so beautiful. Her dress was of some filmy blue material that flared at the hips, and swooped in long, full lines to the very toes of her shoes. Her bonnet was tied beneath her chin with wide, blue ribbons that enhanced the deep brown of her eyes.

"Do you like me in this dress?" she curtsied, her cheeks coloring. "I stopped off in Omaha and bought it."

"You look like a queen," he said gallantly, helping her into the buggy. Actually he felt shabby and a little ashamed in his shiny, brown suit and worn shoes.

Nancy climbed into the buggy, and they were just driving away, when Jim Hart pounded by on a wiry buckskin bronc, and stopped at the livery stable.

"Isn't that your rig that the Parson's got?" he asked of the man in charge.

A wide grin transfigured the fellow's dour expression. "Yeh, and he don't know it, but he just bought hisself a horse. He put up a fifty buck deposit on that mare, and — hee, hee, hee," he mopped the tears from his faded eyes with a dirty handkerchief. "And she's so sick I was scared she'd keel over before I got the harness on her. He'll never make it to North Platte with that nag, I could tell him that."

"Well, he might have a 'nag' in the harness, but he's sure got a couple of right pert fillies in the buggy with him. What'd you say he was goin' to North Platte for?"

"I didn't say, but he told me that he was fixin' to get married."

"Not to both of 'em!" Jim ejaculated.

"I don't know. You never can tell about a Parson."

The cowboy spurred his mount, and was away in a swirl of dust.

* * *

The bridal trio was jolting over the hills towards the county seat. The old mare was toiling through the sand like a turtle going up hill, and Nancy was talking excitedly.

"I sure do like weddings," she said. "Aren't you just the least bit nervous? I wouldn't be able to say, 'I do'."

Martha managed a pasty smile. Her face was radiant, but the palms of her hands were moist, and her fingers persisted in trembling as they knotted and unknotted her handkerchief. "I don't know what there is to be nervous about," she answered.

"No," John agreed. "I—I don't see a thing to be nervous about."

"This is the first time I've ever been a maid of honor," Nancy went on. "You had ought to have got a best man, John. You can't have a proper wedding without a best man."

His face clouded. "I don't have ary a friend in Regina Springs that I'd feel like asking to come along."

"I'm sorry," she said. "I didn't know."

"What's the matter with this horse?" Martha inquired suddenly. "She's acting awful funny."

The mare was acting strange. She was throwing her feet forward, in a desperate effort to remain standing. And her sides were heaving like the bellows on an organ. She stumbled and staggered along for a dozen steps or more, then shuddered, from the tip of her nose to the end of her tail, and collapsed in the harness.

John leaped out of the buggy, but by the time he reached her, she was dead. He straightened, and looked around. Those barren, rounded hills stretched out before the eye, monotonously to the horizon. There wasn't a tree or a building in any direction, nor the sign of any moving thing.

"What are we going to do?" Martha asked, her eyes brimming.

"We haven't passed a house for miles," Nancy put in. "We might have to just light out and walk till we find someone. Isn't this a horrible thing to have happening on a wedding day?"

"You girls stay with the buggy," John said, casting a warning glance to Nancy. "I'll start walking towards North Platte. There's surely a ranch or homestead up here a little ways."

"You're not going to leave us out here in the w-wilderness alone," Martha told him. "If you leave this buggy, Nancy and me are going along with you."

"But you couldn't walk half a mile in them shoes. You'll be safe enough here, and I'll come right back."

"Just the same, we aren't going to stay alone."

While they were arguing there was a rataplan of hoofs behind them, and Jim Hart pulled up beside the buggy. His bronc was fiddle-footing impatiently, and he had to keep jerking at the reins.

"What's the matter, Parson, are you givin' your horse a rest, or did you just stop to talk to these here pretty gals? I don't blame you if you did. They're a couple of beauts." His words may have been insulting, but his voice was plainly complimentary. Nancy flushed. "Which one's yours, Parson?"

John chose to ignore the question, and introduced him to Martha and Nancy. He told the young cowboy of their predicament.

Hart leaned back in the saddle. "I'll make a deal with you, Parson. Let me set up there in front beside this pretty gal, and be best man at your wedding, and I'll get you into town."

"I think that's just too nice for words," Nancy thrilled. "We've been wishing and wishing that we had a best man, all the way from Regina Springs."

"Sounds like that's settled, then." He got down from his horse, and began to take the harness from the dead animal. "Lend me a hand, Parson."

The two of them got the harness loose and the buggy backed away, then Hart went to work on his saddle horse. He got the saddle off easily enough, but harnessing the salty bronc was something different, like trying to snip the rattles from the tail of an aggravated diamond back. The buckskin swapped ends, sunfished, and tried to plant his fore feet into the cowboy's middle. Jim followed him nimbly, avoiding the flashing hoofs. After the third try he succeeded in getting the belly band fastened. In another ten minutes the rest of the harness was in place, and the trembling cow pony submitted to the final straw of indignity in allowing himself to be hitched to the buggy, like a common, ordinary work horse.

Jim climbed gingerly into the seat, braced his feet, and gritted, "Hang on!"

Touching the whip to the frightened horse was like putting a match to the short fuse on a stick of dynamite.

The animal snorted, wild-eyed. His head went down, his tail went up, and he bolted headlong down the rough trail; trying to buck and side-step as best he could, within the narrow confines of the buggy shafts. The buggy snapped and catapulted in a zig-zag course across the deep ruts in the trail, like the thongs of a mule skinner's whip cracking across the rumps of a lead team. It leaped and bounded, careening down hills, and racing along the narrow valleys. It was the wildest, mad-cap ride that John and the girls had ever taken. They clung to their seats like monkeys on a pony's back.

"Stop! Stop!" Nancy chattered.

John and Martha went sprawling to one side, then lurched to the other, as they whipped around the corner and over a short hill. Jim thrilled to the ride like a wrangler topping a bronc.

"This fellow's going to get all the fight taken out of him."

He applied the whip, and the wiry little horse quit trying to buck, and stretched out along the ground in headlong flight. The buggy seemed to fly across the prairie, but the ride was gradually smoother as the pace began to tell on the rapidly exhausting animal. He slowed to a rolling gallop, and at last to a trembling, lathered walk.

"Now," Jim panted, "maybe he'll behave hisself."

"I — I hope so."

The rest of the ride was uneventful. In North Platte they went to a jewelry store to get a ring, then stopped at the court house. It was a bit embarrassing for John. He couldn't find his wallet, and Jim had to pay for the license. After a hurried trip back to the jeweler's he found his money in his inside coat pocket, where it had been all the time.

The ceremony was beautiful in its simplicity. The sun's last rays were slanting through the stained glass figure of

Christ that made up the central theme in the large window at the back of the church; casting shadows and soft streams of light about the empty pews. A pair of tall, white tapers at either side of the pulpit dispelled the shadows, and illumined the solemn faces of the little group.

John and Martha were standing in front of the minister; while Jim was at one side, and Nancy was at the other. Jim's manner had been flippant, but now the sacred atmosphere took the smile from his lips and replaced it with a look that was almost reverent.

Martha's voice was low; she could scarcely be heard above the soft chords of the organ, but John spoke out loud and clear. It was a short service, and in a few moments he was kissing her happily. With the slightest trace of a smile the young cowboy kissed her too. Nancy swept a tear from her eye, and pecked Martha lightly on the cheek. Then they were outside once more.

As they got back into the buggy Jim turned to the Parson. "I never went to a weddin' like that before," he said gravely. "We usually get a couple of kegs of beer and throw a big shindig. This was kind of sacred and happy like."

The moon was lighting the trail when the thoroughly humiliated cow pony succeeded in dragging the buggy back to Regina Springs.

Chapter 7

THE kerosene lamps in Dozbaba's store were lighted, casting an irregular, yellow patch of light on the broken board walk in front. There was a rig at the hitching rail; and Jake Dozbaba was sitting in the doorway, looking uncomfortable in his shiny, tight-fitting blue suit and stiff collar, that gave him a look of being pinched at the neck, like the end of a toy balloon.

Through the window John could see Mrs. Dozbaba, Mrs. Morelin, the homesteading widow, and Belle, in silk finery that had probably lain in their trunks, unused, for a year or two.

The long counter that ran the length of the general store had been moved to one side, and in its place was a table spread for ten or twelve guests. Red and green ribbons of crepe paper were festooned above the table, and red and green paper hearts were placed at each plate. A towering three-layer cake, with the traditional bride and groom standing on the white icing, completed the picture.

"Oh," Nancy squealed, delightedly. "It's a reception."

Martha squeezed John's hand as they got out of the buggy, and paused, while she brushed a tear from the corner of her eye.

"Isn't it beautiful?" she tremored.

At that moment John felt that all the world was with him. Jake got up and came forward to meet them.

"Congratulations, Parson," he said, offering his hand. "Mama and a couple of ladies has fixed a little dinner for you folks. Some other peoples they invited also, but they didn't come, I guess maybe."

Jim Hart would have driven away, but Nancy insisted that he come in.

"Why, you were the best man," she told him. "You can't go traipsing off without going to the reception."

He shook his head. "Them aren't my kind of folks in there."

"I reckon I'd sure like to have you come," she said frankly, her wide gray eyes looking full into his.

Without a word he got out of the buggy and tied the horse to the rail beside the other. Dozbaba was shocked when he saw him, but he managed to be cordial.

Mrs. Dozbaba waddled forward excitedly and kissed Martha damply on both cheeks. Belle grasped her hand, and held it while she talked with her. "Oh, honey, I'm so happy for you," she said. "The Parson's been talkin' about you nearly ever since he came. I hope you have the best of everything."

Mrs. Morelin spoke to Martha, and looked queerly at Jim. She was a nester, while he came from the other side of the fence. Her son, Tom, was even more blunt.

"I ain't going to eat with no lousy cowpoke!" he grated, kicking over his chair, and storming outside.

The incident was a little upsetting, and for a few minutes everyone sat around, looking at each other in strained silence. Then Mrs. Dozbaba came in from the kitchen.

"Well, my goodness, why don't you up by the table set? What's the matter? Aren't you hungry?"

The dinner was one of those elaborate country style affairs, beginning with a steaming platter of fried chicken and a mountainous pile of mashed potatoes, and ending with huge wedges of apple pie. When it was over Jake Dozbaba stood up and cleared his throat.

"And now, we drink a toast to the bride and groom." He held up his coffee cup, and the others did likewise.

At that point there was a sound at the door, and Clara stumbled inside. It was a different Clara than John had ever seen. Her rouge and lipstick was awry, and her straw-colored hair straggled over her eyes, and poked up about her hat, disheveled and unkempt.

"You can't drink a toast with that kind of stuff," she mumbled coarsely. "Here, try this." She tossed an almost empty bottle of whiskey on the table, right on the cake. The bride and groom were knocked to the floor. "So sorry. So sorry." She went over to pick up the figures, and almost fell.

Belle sat there, too horrified to speak. Her face was ashen.

"I just wanted to come down here and kiss the Parson goodby. You don't mind if I kiss the Parson goodby, do you, honey?" She turned to Martha who had flushed scarlet.

Jim got up and took Clara by the shoulders. "Come on, old girl," he said easily. "I think you'd better let me take you home."

She tried to wrench away. "I don't wanna go home, Jimmy boy. I just want to stay here and kiss the Parson."

Belle took hold of her arm, and helped Jim lead her to the door. "I'm awfully sorry this had to happen," she apologized over her shoulder. "I wouldn't have had it happen on your weddin' night for the world."

"You don't need to apologize for me, Belle Williams. The Parson's my boy friend, and I can kiss him if I want to."

"Come on, now. That's enough of that." Jim pushed her, protesting, out the door. A dozen or two grinning, bearded ruffians were crowded onto the porch.

"Look!" Clara announced triumphantly. "Here's some more folks what want to kiss the Parson."

"You'd better take her home alone, Belle," Jim whispered. "I think I'll be needed here."

The men shouldered past them, into the front of the general store. John knew some of them. There was Craig of the Box Bar Y, Hart's partner, the station agent, and a host of saloon habitues. He had seen them come reeling out of the saloons, stupefied with liquor and lack of sleep.

"We heard you got married, Parson," Craig said. "We just came over to wish you luck."

"Thank you, Brother Craig," John said, coming towards them. "I'd like to introduce my wife."

Martha would have stepped up beside him, but Jim Hart took her by the arm, and shook his head.

"Thought maybe we'd bum you for the treats," Julius Hart simpered.

"Yeh, trot out the treats."

John turned a sallow, salmon pink. "Buying treats plumb slipped my mind, but I reckon we can take care of that. Brother Dozbaba, do you have any candy?"

"Sure, candy is one thing I got lots of." He went behind the counter. "But I don't think it's candy that they're talkin' about."

"You're right, Dozy!" Craig blustered, stepping closer to John. "We figured on goin' over to the saloon and havin' *you* set up the drinks!"

"That's out of the question!" He clipped the words short, and turned towards the back of the store. Craig grabbed him and spun him around.

"Oh no you don't, Parson!" he grated. "We come here to get the drinks, and we're goin' to get them!"

"What are you doin' here?" Julius Hart demanded of Jim.

"That's none of your business."

"We'll give them a charivari that they won't never forget!" one of them shouted. "Grab the bride!"

"I got her!" Jim Hart answered. With that he grasped Nancy about the waist and pushed her out the door ahead of him. Before anyone could protest he had put her in the buggy and driven away.

"And what is this all about, Mister Hart?" she demanded primly.

"Them fellows is bad hombres when they're drunk." He slowed the horse to a walk and settled back into the seat comfortably. "There's no telling what they might do to Martha if they was to get hold of her."

"What's that got to do with dragging me around like you owned me?" Her voice was edged with ice.

Jim laughed pleasantly. "Well, you see, Nancy darlin', them guys don't know which girl the Parson married. They'll figure it's you, no matter what those other folks tell them. And why should I spend a beautiful moonlight night like this riding around with somebody else's wife? Especially when there's a pretty little filly like you runnin' around without no brand?"

"I reckon I've got to ride with you," she retorted sharply. "But I don't have to talk to you."

He dropped the reins and looked at her. "I'm right sorry I made you mad, Nancy. But the truth of it is, I'd rather just ride beside you, than to kiss any other girl I know."

In spite of herself, she smiled.

While back at Dozbaba's store Craig was saying, "Didn't no one go with them?"

"Nope."

John glared at him.

"Well, let's get goin'. We'll find Jim after while."

Craig gave John a shove towards the door, and he stumbled, almost sprawling on the walk outside. The night was a torment. They were all drunk, and disgustingly insulting. They took him out into the hills west of Regina Springs.

"Here's where you walk, Parson!"

"Get down, and we'll take you to meet your bride."

"I tell you my wife's back at the store."

"Don't give us none of that stuff."

They forced him off the horse, and made him scramble up the steepest hills that they could find, over shifting white sand blow-outs and rough ground, alike. Craig and Julius Hart rode on either side, prodding him with their guns when he didn't go fast enough. Once, when he got ten paces ahead, Hart roped him and yanked him to the ground.

"Maybe we had ought to take him back to his bride now, what say, fellows?"

"Might be a good idea."

He was bundled onto the swayed-back horse, and they rode for several miles to an abandoned ranch house.

"Now, isn't that funny?" Craig said. "I'd have swore Jimmy would have brung her here."

They took him to another, and yet another place; cuffing and knocking him around like a calf at branding time. As the hours passed they became more surly and angry.

"Maybe we'd be able to find her if the Parson was to buy us a little refreshment. We can't think real hard on a empty stomach."

"Yeh, I bet we would. A fellow gits awful dry in this here night air."

"What say, Parson. Would you like to see your bride?"

"You've had your fun. Why don't you let me go home?" John demanded through swollen lips.

"You'll get to go home when you take us in and buy us a round of drinks. Not before."

The temptation to yield was great. One trouser leg had been ripped off, and the other was split from the cuff to the knee. Blood from a cut on his cheek had trickled down over the collar of his white shirt, leaving a jagged, brownish path. His eye was swollen shut, and his arms and legs were scratched and bleeding.

They were drinking more frequently now, from a seemingly inexhaustible supply of whiskey in Craig's saddle bags. The third bottle had already been emptied, and they were on the fourth. One more drink wouldn't make any difference to them. They were drunk anyway. Besides, he'd taken more punishment now than anyone had a right to expect one man to absorb.

"Would you give me your word that you'd let me go home, if I was to buy you the drinks?" The words scalded his mouth, leaving an acrid, unclean taste.

"Sure would. Now you're talkin' sense, Parson. That's the kind of a preacher we want, one that's reasonable. We'll get along fine from here on out, if you just act reasonable."

"I thought he was just handing us a line, with all that high and mighty stuff. I guessed it from the start. Just as soon as I heard where he was living at, I knowed he couldn't be so all-fired pious."

"Yeh, and I guess that kind of shows what kind of a girl he married, too."

John clenched his fist, and would have struck Craig, but the others swarmed onto him, and pinned his arms to his sides.

"Oh, so you want to play, do you? Let's bounce all the play out of him."

They threw him on the ground. Two men grabbed his legs, and two his arms. "One—two—three!" They bounced him in unison, and at the last count, threw him high in the air. He spread-eagled, turned over once, and thudded to the ground. His left arm doubled under him, and an involuntarily groan escaped his lips.

"Come on there! Get up!" Craig kicked him in the side, but he didn't move.

One of the Box Bar Y cowboys, Shorty Florell, knelt beside him, and turned him over. "He's hurt. We'd better get him to a doctor."

That sobered them somewhat, and a couple lifted him onto a horse. Shorty sat behind the saddle and held him on. The rest of the crowd scattered.

In town the doctor examined him carefully.

"His arm's got a bad break," he said, "just below the elbow. And to make it worse, it was compounded bringing him here. It's a good thing it wasn't a bit higher, or we'd have a man with a stiff arm."

Martha cried when she saw him, lying so white and still on a cot in the doctor's office. Belle stood with her arm about her.

"He'll be all right, honey. In the morning we'll move him out to my place, and you and Nancy and the Parson can stay there till he get's well."

"B-b-but we haven't any money," she sobbed.

"Don't you worry about that now. You just think about helpin' the Parson get back on his feet as soon as he can. He's got a heap of work to do."

Chapter 8

MARTHA kept a constant vigil over him during the night, holding his right hand, and wiping his forehead with a damp cloth. He slept restlessly, groaning and tossing with pain, and calling for her if she moved away from the bed for a moment. At three o'clock Nancy came over with a pot of steaming hot coffee, and insisted that she drink it and lie down for a few minutes. At five, the doctor came toddling in, in his night shirt and slippers, to check the splints and take the patient's pulse.

After breakfast he was feeling better. Dull, throbbing pains still racked his arm and shoulder whenever he moved, but he felt quite comfortable when lying still. About noon they took him out to Belle's in Jake Dozbaba's spring wagon. It was a tortuous ride, though Jake was as careful as possible. The wagon jounced over the rough streets, stabbing white-hot slivers up and down his arm, and his whole side ached when they finally arrived. Jim Hart was waiting at the boarding house, and helped carry him upstairs to the bed that Martha and Belle had fixed for him.

Jim stayed beside the bed until the Bohemian storekeeper excused himself. "Here's a little present for you, Parson," he said, tossing a small roll of bills onto the bed. "Bill Bruer, down at the livery barn, decided he wasn't going to keep your deposit money after all. He sent these fifty simoleons back to you."

"That was right good of him, now wasn't it? He wouldn't have had to done it, neither. I didn't bring back his horse."

"I didn't exactly say that he wanted to. You see, I had to kind of persuade him a little."

The Parson looked at him strangely. "Why did you do that, Brother Hart? I bargained to bring back his horse and buggy, and I didn't do it."

"He shouldn't never have lent that animal out in the first place. He bragged to me that she was so sick he was afeered she'd die before he got the harness on her, and had turned her over to you."

"Well, now, why do you reckon he'd want to do a thing like that? I never done anything to him."

"Just your comin' here was enough to make him hate you. Bill don't have nothing to do with no church, or anyone who does."

"I do want to thank you, Brother Hart, for getting the money back for me. It's going to help tide me and Martha over a right rough spell. I sure wish I was able to pay you for your trouble."

"Forget it," Hart said shortly. "And don't give me no more of that 'Brother Hart' stuff. When you say that, I don't even know who you're talkin' to." He started to go, then turned back. "You know, Parson, that Nancy's about the nicest and prettiest gal I ever did meet."

John smiled.

When Jim was gone Martha came in. "How are you feeling, honey?" she asked, kissing him.

"All right, I guess."

When he showed her the money that Jim had brought to him, her face brightened; then, like the sun when blotted out by scurrying clouds, darkened again.

"That was a terrible thing that happened last night," she said. "I'm afraid for you. Do you suppose we could get another charge? One where the people aren't so wild and wicked?"

"The wicked places is the places that *need* the Word of God. We can't leave, Martha. If we did, there wouldn't be no one left to carry on."

"I know, honey. I'm sorry for even suggesting such a thing. It'll be tol'able hard, but we'll carry on."

John didn't answer her. He was lying still and expressionless on the bed, as though he hadn't even heard what she said.

"There's something bothering you, John. Are you worried about me?"

He started. "I'm sorry, dear. What did you say?"

"Are you worrying about me?"

"In a way, yes, but that ain't what I been thinking about right now. I been lying here wondering if I'm *fit* to preach here, or any place else."

"Fit to be preaching? Why, John Woodring, I'm ashamed of you. How can you say a think like that? After standing up to them the way you did last night when they wanted you to buy drinks. I was that proud of you!"

"I didn't stand up to 'em, Martha. Not all the time, I didn't." He had to force out the words. "They run me, and cussed me, and knocked me around till I told them *I'd buy a round of drinks,* if they'd only take me back to town."

"Oh." A little cry escaped her lips.

"If I had got to do it we'd have been finished here in Regina Springs. Even them saloon bums wouldn't have no respect for me," he sighed. "The only thing that saved me, I reckon, was me breaking my arm."

Martha looked at him as though she wanted to gather him close to her, like a penitent child. "You should ought to thank God that He didn't let you go through with it."

"Do you suppose that was why my arm was broke?" he queried thoughtfully.

"I couldn't answer that, dear. It's not for us to decide what comes of God and what doesn't."

"I reckon you're right." He shifted his position slightly, and winced with pain.

Martha got up and came close to the bed. "Can I get you something, John?"

He shook his head. "It's better now. I reckon I had the wrong idea when I come out here. I was filled with the fire of the Lord, thinking that these people were anxious to have a church. I was going to give them a church, *alone,* if I had to. I'd been boasting to myself about how *I* was going to do so much, and at the first real test I failed myself, and the church, and God."

"There's not any of us that're perfect, John darling." She rubbed her hand over his forehead soothingly. "I'd probably done the same thing, quicker than you did, if I'd been in your place. If you made a mistake, it was in trusting yourself too much, and not trusting *God* enough. We'll just have to have a little more faith and trust the next time."

He grasped her hand and squeezed it tightly.

"Now don't worry about it no more," she said. "Go to sleep awhile if you can."

John smiled and closed his eyes.

* * *

He improved rapidly, and it wasn't long until he was coming downstairs for his meals. In a few days he spent the

afternoons in the large leather upholstered rocker in Belle
and Clara's parlor. Though he never mentioned her con-
duct at the store, Clara avoided him pointedly. Whenever
he was in the same room, she was fidgity and uncomfortable; and, whenever she felt his eyes upon her, her face
colored. She was even more petulant around Martha, and
there were times when a look came into her eyes that was
closely akin to hatred. Belle may have suspected the reason,
but wasn't sure until one day just before the Parson was
able to come down for his meals.

"Would you take this soup up to the Parson?" she said.
"I've got to set the table for that gang o' wolves that'll be
here any minute now."

"Is *she* up there?" Clara's voice was bitter.

"And who'd have a better right to be with the Parson
than his wife?" Belle paried, her keen eyes probing deep
into Clara's heart.

"I don't care if she's got a right or not. I'm not goin' up
and have them snake eyes of hers follering me, and watching every move I make."

"You're in love with the Parson, ain't you, Clara?" She
shot the question abruptly.

"And what if I am? There's no law agin it."

"He's another woman's husband now, Clara."

Clara dropped into a chair at the table, and threw her
head into her arms, sobbing. Belle put an arm awkwardly
about her, and tried to comfort her. But through the years
of bickering and sin, they had never been close to each
other; and the barrier that had been built slowly through
the years kept Belle from helping Clara now. Gradually the
sobbing subsided, but the tears continued to flow, streaking
her powder. The sacs beneath her eyes were red and
swollen.

"I've knowed he never thought nothing of me," she said, after the crying stopped. "But it never done no good. I'm still crazy about him. I think I've loved him ever since I saw him defyin' those roughnecks who tried to make him stop asking a blessing. And then, when we saw him in that building preaching to empty rows of seats, that finished it."

"I understand just what you're goin' through, Clara."

"Oh no you don't," her voice showed a trace of hardness once more. "I'd do anything to get the Parson for my own. I think I'd have even become a Christian."

"The Parson told me that there's only one kind of real Christian — those who come to Him because they repent their sins, and love Him for Himself," Belle said gently. "Why don't *you* try *Him,* Clara. He'll help you over these hard days."

"Hmph! I'm not worth it."

"Please?"

"Nope." She got up and surveyed her tear-stained face in the mirror. "You'll have to find some other sucker to do your preaching to. I'm going up and put on some more war paint."

After that Clara took to drinking more and more frequently, until her mind seemed befogged most of the time, and her eyes became glazed and blood-shot.

The men at the boarding house acted with remarkable restraint when Martha and Nancy were present. They took to washing for dinner, and one or two even put on clean shirts and neckties before coming down to eat.

Regularly every night, one or another asked Nancy to go out with him, and, just as regularly, she refused. Only Jim Hart succeeded in dating her, and the others were openly envious of him. Nancy got exasperated with him and his frankness, or attempts at flattery — she hadn't been able to decide which. But, in spite of that, she found herself looking forward to his visits, and being disappointed when he didn't come. It wasn't often that he disappointed her, for he was over as often as he could get away from the ranch.

By the end of the second week John was well enough to move into a place of their own, and he and Martha began to look for a house. They found a small, vacant sod house across the street from Belle's. It was a neat, three-room structure with board floors and plastered walls and ceiling. The windows were small, and set well back into the thick dirt walls, but, aside from that, it looked as nice as any home from within. And in Regina Springs the exterior of a building didn't matter.

Belle loaned them a little furniture, and Dozbaba let them use an old cook stove and a bed that had been collecting dust and dirt in his woodshed for several years. The balance of the furniture they bought.

Belle came over and helped Martha and Nancy scrub the floors and put up the curtains; and Jim brought the stove from Dozbaba's and set it up. The Parson still wasn't much help, managing to get in the way more than anything else.

Of course Nancy moved with them. They made a bed for her on the duo-fold in their front room, and fixed a rack in one corner of the small bedroom on which to hang their clothes.

That evening Nancy showed John and Martha a letter that she had received from her parents at noon.

"Paw's finishing his work in the hills," she said. "And they are planning on sending him out here in western Nebraska some place to help with organizin' work."

"We could use some one like that here, couldn't we, John dear?" Martha cried excitedly. "I've heard Nancy's Paw sing, and he's wonderful! Why don't you write the super-intendent and see if he'll get the Bishop to send the Rileys here to help us for three or four weeks. Interest has kind of died down here, and some real good singing would pack in the crowds. You'd ought to have seen how they flocked in to hear him down home."

"I reckon I'll write to Bishop King myself," he said after awhile. "I've got to report to him how the work is going, anyway."

The next morning he wrote the letter and ventured up-town to mail it. It was the first time that he'd gone out in public since the night of the charivari. He felt conspicuous with his arm in a sling; and wanted to avoid people on the street, but that was impossible. As he went past the general store Mrs. Dozbaba thrust her head out the door.

"How are you feeling, Parson? So happy we are to see you. You will be starting the church once more soon, maybe?"

"Yes, Sister Dozbaba, we'll be starting pretty soon now."

He could feel the eyes of the passersby upon him. Some of them looked sympathetically, but the others only smirked.

He had no sooner left the portly matron than the bar-tender came dashing out of the saloon and accosted him.

"You're wanted inside, Parson, quick!" the fellow panted.

John looked at him sharply. "Is this a joke?"

"Honest, Parson! A guy just cashed in. They want you inside right away."

He hesitated a moment. The crowd in there was against him. They had done everything possible to make Regina Springs intolerable. He shouldn't stop. And yet, if some-one had died, he had no right to question the motives of those who called on him. This might be the opening wedge to their hearts.

He followed the bartender down the walk, and through the bat-wing doors into the saloon. There was a rough pine box in the middle of the floor, and the men were standing somberly about with their hats in their hands.

John took off his hat and stepped closer to look down into the rough box. It was a miserable sight. The poor fellow was a tattered, unshaven derelict about forty-five or fifty years old. His graying hair, tangled and uncombed, bushed out over his ears; and his mouth was open slightly, revealing two blackened snags that looked like anything but the teeth that they were. His eyes were closed.

"What did you want me to do?" John's voice was hushed.

"We'd like to have you preach a sermon for poor old Fred. Would you do that for us?" Hart said, his voice matching John's in reverence.

John looked about, at the long mahogany bar and the row upon row of liquors behind it, at the gaming tables that were scattered about the rest of the room, and the lewd paintings that lined the walls.

"This isn't a very good place for a funeral. Wouldn't you like to take him up the street to the church? It'd be a lot better, I think."

"No sir, Fred lived here and drank here. We think he'd ought to be buried from here."

"You won't have to have him embalmed, J. C.," one of the men wise-cracked. "He's already pickled." Laughter skittered over the crowd.

John took a small testament from his pocket and read a bit of scripture. It was probably the first time that many of his listeners had ever heard any portion of the Bible.

There was a satirical grin on Julius Hart's face, and Craig and one or two of the others were ad-libbing under their breath. Those standing close by snickered at intervals. But John went on as though he were before a respectful audience.

There in the sawdust, with the stench of stale whiskey reeking in his nostrils, he began his sermon. It was an impromptu talk, without beginning or end, that would probably have brought sneers of criticism from his more learned contemporaries. But it electrified his listeners. The laughter was swept from their faces as they stood, open-mouthed, while a slight, red-haired minister challenged them. This was no sermon of sweet-sounding platitudes. It came down to their level, slugging through their rough exteriors to the barren, filthy souls beneath.

"God gave each of us a body in His own likeness," he said. "And He's given us minds and souls that're intended to glorify Him. Some try to do that very thing, but there are many who don't. Instead, they've wrecked their bodies, drugged their minds, and lost their souls through their own ignorant worshiping of that *demon,* Rum.

"I reckon this poor fellow died in a drunken stupor. If that's right, then every man in this saloon today is partly to blame for his death. Think of that a minute!" He turned to Hart and took a step towards him. "Think of that, Julius Hart! You helped to kill a man! You helped to kill him for the profit you made on the whiskey he drank. And you," he addressed the bartender. "You served the liquor that killed him for the wages you get." The saloon owner's face turned purple with rage, and the bartender stepped back, as though he'd been struck in the face at the accusation. The others were scowling fiercely.

"I reckon maybe it's worse for the rest of you. You've got nothing at all to show for your part. You've got nothing but the ruination of your own souls. But your share in the murder is just as big as Hart's. From the looks of this poor man in the rough box he was just a bum, hanging around the saloon for the drinks you gave him.

"He's dead, but the thing that killed him still lives, like a rattlesnake lying in wait for some other victim. That's the charge against you. *Your* business has kept this place open in the past. *It caused this man's death!* And your business will keep it open in the future, unless you come face to face with yourselves, and realize how rotten your lives have been. Unless you come to realize that you're steeped in sin, and feel the *need* of Jesus Christ, you are lost; and this whole town's future is placed in jeopardy."

He lowered his voice, and the room was strangely quiet. "I could tell you of the wonders of Jesus. I could tell you how He can change your lives, and make you fine and clean and good. You've all seen Belle Williams. You know that she was living in sin before she accepted Jesus as her personal Saviour. And you know how she's *changed*. You know what He can do for you if you will let Him."

"In that rough box is a man that you, and you, and you, helped to kill. Except for the grace of God, *you* might be lying there in his place."

The fellow in the rough box blinked his bloodshot eyes, shook his head, and sat up stupidly. "Say, what's goin' on here anyway? Has anybody got a drink? Give me a drink! Somebody give me a drink!"

Laughter swept over the crowd, but it was a strained attempt, sputtering and going out like a wet fuse. He faced the malevolent glare of some twenty-five or thirty angry drunks.

It had all been a joke. He was probably dead drunk most of the time. They had just waited until the Parson came along the street and put him in the rough box. John's hair-trigger temper skyrocketed.

"I see this was supposed to be a joke!" he began angrily. "But you aren't laughing like you figured you would. And I can tell you why. It's because your joke back-fired. You stand, convicted, before God and your fellowmen. It don't matter that this fellow's not really dead, for he is dead spiritually, just like the rest of you. I wonder if you realize how he symbolized all of you when he was lying in that box?" John paused while his words drove home.

"I'm glad you gave me this chance to talk to you, though I'd rather have had it under a little different circumstances. I only pray that you men'll think of what I have tried to tell you, and accept Jesus before it is too late. He offers you the only salvation possible!"

They stood there in stunned silence. Even Hart seemed paralyzed, struck speechless by the force of his words.

"If any of you want to come to church you'll be more than welcome." With that he stalked regally out of the saloon, unharmed.

Chapter 9

JOHN went on up the street to mail the letter, his feet pounding out a rhythmic tattoo on the board walk. Hot blood tingled in his fingertips and blazed to a white heat in his cheeks. He stared without seeing, straight ahead. A homesteader's wife, who was standing on the corner, spoke to him pleasantly; and he grunted in answer as he passed, not even noting who she was.

They had made a fool of him at the saloon. That fact jarred through his mind with every step. That much he could stand, for he had become used to ridicule since moving to Regina Springs. But they had done more than that in mocking him. They had mocked a sacred ritual, the church, and God.

Perhaps some of them had been touched by his message. They were certainly shocked enough by it. If there had been any indication, there in the saloon, that even one might accept Christ, he'd have stayed; but the atmosphere was one of tense expectancy, like the moment before taking the blindfold from the eyes of a saddled outlaw stallion. Every one of them looked as though he would have helped to tar and feather the Parson, if only someone had made the first move. In that moment of indecision John had left.

This time he had walked from among them, unharmed, but the next he might not be so fortunate. They'd try again soon, under the goad of revenge. There was no need of denying it to himself, he was frightened at the thought of facing them. They were capable of anything.

It would do no good to tell Martha what had happened. There was nothing that she could do to change things, and she'd only worry about him.

But the moment he stepped into the house, that resolution vanished. She sensed that something was wrong and followed him into the bedroom, sat down beside him on the bed, and entwined her arm about his waist.

"What's the matter, darling?"

"It's nothing to worry about," he said off-handedly. "Is supper ready?"

"You know it isn't, John," she said softly. "You were through the kitchen only a minute ago." Her eyes caught his boring into the floor, and lifted them forcibly. "You didn't answer my question, dear."

"It's really nothing, just a little fracas up town that sort of upset me."

"You'd feel a sight better if you was to tell me."

"It wasn't anything, Martha. Let's just forget all about it. Where's Nancy?"

"She's over to Belle's. Now, won't you tell me about it?"

"All right," he grinned. "I reckon I'll have to tell you if there's to be any peace in the family. It was this-away . ." He told her everything except of his own fears for what might happen the next day, or the next, or maybe that very night.

"*This* time you showed them," she said proudly when he finished.

He pulled her close, and kissed her.

"I've got to go now. It's time for supper, and Nancy's got company coming tonight."

"Jim Hart?"

"And who else would it be? She's getting that look in her eyes," Martha laughed.

"I like Jim, but I wish she wouldn't be so friendly with him."

"Jim's a good boy, John. A body can't blame him for being like he is. He just hasn't had no raising, that's all." Martha was peeling potatoes, and John got some wood from the box beside the stove and awkwardly tried to build the fire. "Here, let me do that," she said.

"I reckon I'm not a cripple," he protested. Nevertheless he backed away from the range. "It isn't that I don't think Jim's a good boy. In a lot of ways he is. And he's sure helped us a heap. But he isn't the kind of a fellow Nancy had ought to marry."

"I can't help thinking you're wrong, John."

"I don't believe she'd ever marry a non-Christian, and I don't reckon he'll ever be converted."

Martha put the potatoes on the stove and bustled over to the cupboard to get a slab of salt pork. "You just give Nancy time. I'm reckoning she'll fetch him around to her way of thinking, before long."

"Might be, but that's something he's got to decide for hisself. And he can't just say that he's a Christian to make her happy. He's got to *believe*."

At that point Nancy came in. Her face was flushed and her eyes sparkled excitedly. "Oh, Martha, it's going to be the prettiest dress you ever did see. Belle's fixing it all full of ruffles, and tucks, and it's got a flounce on the skirt and — "

"And you hope Jim likes you in it," Martha added laughingly.

"Oh, you! Quit teasing me, Martha Woodring. You know Jim and me's just friends." The blush in her cheeks belied her words. "Just for that I won't give you this letter that come over to Belle's this afternoon."

"A letter for me?" Martha dropped the salt pork on the table and went over to her. "Let me see it."

Nancy held it, tantalizing, out of reach. "I didn't fetch it over for you. It's John's."

"What's his is mine, and what's mine is my own. Come on, *please* let me see it."

"I reckon I hadn't ought to. It's in a woman's handwriting, looks like. It might be from a old sweetheart or something."

"John never had any old sweethearts."

"That's just what he's been telling you. I know better."

"Aw now, cut it out you two," he drawled good naturedly. "You shouldn't talk about a fellow that-away, especially when his back's turned."

"You read it and tell her who it's from," Nancy handed him a long white envelope. "Better think fast, Parson Woodring. You might be in trouble if you don't."

"Why, it's postmarked Omaha," he exclaimed. "It must be from the Bishop."

"I'm going in to get dressed," Nancy announced, while John hurriedly tore open the letter. "Go ahead and question him, Martha. Make him show it to you." Martha laughed, and went out into the kitchen. There was a knock at the door and Nancy thrust her head from behind the bedroom curtain. "If that's Jim, tell him I'll be out in a minute."

John started when he saw who was at the door. He drew back involuntarily as though to close it, then managed to say, "Good evenin', Brother Hart, won't you come in?"

"Don't mind if I do." Julius Hart clomped into the dining room and sat down unceremoniously, on a hard, straight-backed chair beside the table. "What I got to say ain't goin' to take long."

"I'll be out right away, Jim," Nancy sang from the bedroom. "Sit down and visit with John, won't you?"

"This ain't Jim!" He snapped, his voice harsh and rasping. He turned to John. "You wasn't expecting me, was you, Parson."

John shifted a little uneasily, and his right hand trembled as he tugged at the sling, but his voice was firm and even. "I reckoned you'd be around, but I sort of figured you wouldn't come without your friends."

"Are you meaning to say I'm scared of you?" J. C. blustered, his huge fists knotting until the knuckles showed white. He half raised from his chair.

John could feel that Martha and Nancy were listening tensely, and he hoped that they would stay out of the room until the visitor left. The big man's courage had been amply bolstered by strong liquids and talk at the saloon, and he was spoiling for a fight.

"I didn't mean to say that you were scared of me."

Hart settled back into the chair reluctantly. "The boys didn't like the way you talked to them this afternoon, Parson," his lips curled sarcastically over the word.

"I reckon they didn't, Brother Hart."

"They're pretty much worked up over the whole deal. You riled them plenty preaching like that. They're wanting to chase you out of town!" He waited a moment for the words to have their effect. "I guess that's what we ought to do. Chase you plumb out of the county! And your wife, too! I hope they ain't too rough with her, but *you* know how they are when they get riled."

John felt his stomach turn over, and chill to a ball of ice. His free hand grasped the chair arm.

"Yes, I know how they are. I reckon they done about everything to us they can," he said. "But they'll have to chase us out! That's certain! We're going to build a church here, God willing, in spite of anything you, or Craig, or anyone else does. If you chase us away, someone else'll come to take our place and finish the job. This town's going to be opened to Christ!"

Hart got up and towered over the Parson menacingly. "I could smash you to a pulp right now, if I was a mind to!"

John stared blandly into his eyes, though his own heart was thumping like a frightened deer's. "I don't doubt that you could, but *you can't keep me from preaching the Word of God!*"

The saloon owner sat back down and leaned forward confidentially. "You've got spunk, kid, and I like you for it. We don't want to have no trouble with you. You talked sensible just before that accident the other night. You can get along just dandy here in Regina Springs, if you don't get too rambunctious."

"Even God's anointed sin at times. With His help, I ain't going to weaken again."

"Just listen to me a minute, Parson, before you go shootin' off your mouth. You and your wife want a church here, don't you?"

"Of course we do."

"If you'll just listen to reason I'll get you a church. I been thinkin' that, if I put the proposition up to the boys, we might be able to collect enough money to build a church, and give it to you, lock, stock, and barrel."

Without asking, John knew what the price would be. He wouldn't be able to preach any more stirring sermons against drink and gambling. He wouldn't be able to say or do a thing against Hart and his men. Yet the offer was tempting. He and Martha would be free from worry about being pestered, or hurt by drunken hoodlums, and the church could do some good, even under those conditions. Besides, he was tired of fighting.

Martha came to the doorway. The faint yellow glow from the lamp close by deepened the color in her face, and played, like a halo, on her dark hair. She was watching him, as though she knew exactly what was going on in his mind. There was no doubt about what her eyes were telling him.

"I'm sorry that I can't accept your kindness, Brother Hart," he answered. "Under the conditions, I don't reckon it'd be the thing to do. When we build a church it's got to be with Christian money, and on Christian principles. You look like an honest man, and you could be a fine church man. It ain't too late, Brother. Won't you accept Christ?"

"Now don't go pullin' that stuff on me!" Hart jumped to his feet. "If you don't play ball with us now," he cursed, "you will before we get done with you. You might think the boys was rough before, but just you wait!" He jammed his hat onto his head and stormed out the door.

On the steps he met Jim.

"Where do you think you're goin'?" he demanded belligerently.

"I'm going to see Nancy," Jim retorted. "But I been lookin' for you. I want to have a little talk with you."

"And I want to have a talk with you. What's the big idea runnin' with this kind of trash?"

"Because I happen to like it. Have you got any objections?"

"By grab, yes!"

"Do you think it'll do you any good?"

"It'd better, or I'll knock your teeth clean down your throat."

"Try it! I *dare* you to try it!"

"You're a stubborn brat, Jim."

"I come by it natural. I'm goin' in right now, so if you got anything you want to start, you'd better be gettin at it."

"Jim, boy, don't go in. She's nothing but a ———"

Before he could finish the sentence Jim Hart grasped him by the shirt collar and hauled him close with a sledge-like fist. Julius was big, but Jim was even bigger. "Don't say it, Paw, or I'll bash you in two!"

The door opened and Nancy stepped onto the porch. "Hello, Jim," she said gaily. "John was just telling me that your Paw was out here talking to you." She walked directly to Julius and smiled, "I'm right happy to meet your Paw, Jim. How do you do, Mr. Hart."

"G-glad to know you, ma'am," J. C. spluttered. "Jimmy and me was just talking about you."

"I hope it was nice," she dimpled. "Supper's about ready, Jim. And we don't want to keep Martha waiting. Won't you come in too, Mr. Hart? There's plenty for all of us."

"N-no, thank you. I got to be going." He started up the walk, then turned. "I'm right glad to know you, ma'am."

"When you're out this way, Mr. Hart, I'd be right proud to have you stop in and visit a spell."

Without answering, he stalked on up the road. Jim stared after him sullenly.

"I suppose you heard what we said just now."

"Yes," she replied softly. "I heard it."

"I hate him!" he spat. "I know why you done this just now. You done it to keep us from fighting. Well, it wouldn't have been the first time we fought, and it won't be the last. I don't take nothin' from nobody! And especially Paw!"

"We'd better go in, dear. Supper's getting cold."

The meal was hardly a success. They dawdled over their food, as though the events that had just happened had stolen their appetites. There were brief flurries of conversation, and strained laughter, followed by long, embarrassing periods of silence. Finally it was over, and Jim and Nancy went out for a ride.

"Nancy's got a job in her hands," John said solemnly. "That boy's got a wild strain in him, like a mountain lion."

Martha nodded.

"You know, I haven't read that letter from the Bishop." He got up and walked over to the buffet. "I reckon things happened so fast that I plumb forgot it." His face clouded as he read. Awkwardly he sat down, and went over the letter a second time, and then a third. His lips followed the words.

"What's the matter, dear? Bad news?"

He handed her the letter and she read aloud:

"My Dear Brother Woodring:

"It is with a great deal of regret that I write this letter, and only after considerable thought and prayer. I had hoped that we would be able to establish a church in Regina Springs, but I didn't anticipate so much difficulty. From your reports I have come to the conclusion that the money we are spending there could better be used in some more fertile field. I have contacted your superintendent, and he feels the same as I do. Perhaps at some future date when more settlers come into the area, we will try again.

"I have a church just east of Omaha that needs a pastor. It is well established, with a new church and parsonage, and an active congregation. Their minister passed to his reward last month, and they are eager to get an earnest young man to fill the pulpit. I'm sure it would be to your liking, and that they would be pleased with you.

"With kindest personal regards to yourself and bride, I remain, Yours in service,

BISHOP JONATHAN M. KING."

Martha folded the letter and handed it back to John. "Do you want to go?"

"It would be nice to have a church again, and folks to preach to." He beat a tattoo on the table with his fingers. The clock on the wall struck nine o'clock. When the last chime had sounded he said belligerently, "But I don't want to leave. I can't let them run me out of town!"

"If that's your only reason for staying, we'd better go," Martha retorted sharply. "If we're only thinking of ourselves we'll have it a whole lot easier in this other place. But if we're thinking of the good we can do, if we're thinking of the children like Dozbaba's that we can start on the road to Christianity, and make this town safe for them to live in, that's a different matter."

"You want to stay, don't you, darling?"

"No," she said honestly. "I want to go. I want to live in a nice home in a clean town as much as any woman, I reckon. But in spite of what Bishop King says, I feel that God has sent us here!"

John walked into the bedroom alone. There, in the quiet and darkness, he got to his knees to pray. The clock in the dining room struck the quarter hour, the half, and again at ten before he finished. Martha closed her Bible when he came back into the room, and looked up at him questioningly.

"I'm going to write Bishop King and our superintendent," he announced in a hushed voice. "And see if they'll let us stay."

Chapter 10

JOHN had hoped that everyone would be back to church with renewed interest, now that he had moved from the Williams' place, and Belle was astonishing the town with her complete reversal of character. But such wasn't the case. Less than a dozen turned out for prayer meeting on Wednesday evening, and only a few more than that came Sunday. If they had all sat together, less than three rows of seats in the narrow building would have been filled, but they scattered about the room like beans spilling from a sack.

During the week he and Martha borrowed Dozbaba's team and traveled endlessly over the surrounding hills, calling on ranchers and nesters alike. At some places they were welcomed whole-heartedly, while at others a subdued undercurrent of antagonism flowed close to the surface in the conversation. But, in general, they encountered a heartbreaking indifference.

Clay Banter, a homesteader whose land adjoined Morelin's, typified the attitude. "Yeh, we'll be in to church Sunday, Parson," he said, "if it don't rain, and we get the chores done in time. You know it's mighty handy to get around to doing the chores on Sunday morning."

Every night Martha and John prayed fervently that God might let them remain in Regina Springs. The longer that they prayed, the deeper became the calm assurance that He wished them to stay. Confidently they went about planning for the future. Nevertheless, they watched the mails, and when a letter did come from Bishop King, John's hand trembled, and Martha quit drying dishes and stood with bated breath as he opened it.

The Bishop had decided that, against his own personal judgment, he would allow John to stay in Regina Springs for another month, and grant his request to send the Rileys out to help. At the end of that time, however, if they didn't have a congregation sufficiently organized to assure definite results, the town would have to be abandoned.

John read the letter aloud, and as he did so the old enthusiasm lit his features. It was the kind of enthusiasm that had driven him to study long hours when he was so tired that he could scarcely keep awake. Later it had sent him eagerly over the circuit in the Ozarks, where he made scarcely enough to keep himself clothed and fed.

"We'll *make* a place for Christ in this town, Martha," he said.

"I knew it was God's will that we stay here."

John was more excited than Nancy about her parents' coming. He made arrangements, once more, for the room at Dozbaba's, and had some handbills struck off, announcing the opening of Revival Meetings. In large bold type the bills proclaimed, "A GOSPEL MESSAGE IN SONG. Featuring REV. CLIFTON R. RILEY, lyric tenor (The singing evangelist). Beginning Monday, August 17, 1899. Free admission."

He spread the bills indiscriminately over the countryside, leaving them at the homes he called on, tacking them onto store buildings, and handing them to those he met on the street. He smiled when he saw a group of men clustered about one of the bills that was tacked to Dozbaba's General Store. Someone was laboriously reading it aloud. There would be no lack of an audience at their first meeting.

Very few talented entertainers wandered into the sand-hills of Nebraska, and those who did were accorded a royal reception. Belle had told him of a troupe of fifth rate vaude-ville actors who featured a broken-down, black-faced comed-ian. Ranchers drove fifty miles just to see them. That was two years before, and they hadn't had any sort of programs since. John was counting strongly on the desire for enter-tainment to pack the little church building every night.

Nancy's parents arrived on the Monday local from North Platte, and Mr. Riley and John began at once to plan the week's services. They decided that the first meeting was to be one of song entirely.

"I'll sing some good old familiar hymns, Brother Wood-ring," Mr. Riley said, "And we'll get the crowd to join in on the choruses. It helps a heap to break down the stiffness and make everyone friendly. We'll make them a happy, agreeable crowd, first off."

"I reckon we could use a lot of that good feeling here," John said. "There's trouble brewing over land in these parts, and it's getting worse right along. But, I'll tell you about that when we aren't so busy." He pulled out his watch and looked at it. "I know you're tired from riding all night, but I think it would do a tol'able lot of good if I was to take you around and introduce you to some of the men that we can depend on."

"There's no time to start, like right now, I reckon." Mr. Riley was a short, roly-poly man who looked as though he might have been a circus clown, a good natured drummer, or most anything except the evangelist that he actually was. His brown eyes rode majestically on either side of his broad beamed nose, and protruded a little, to give his face a some-what grotesque appearance. His bald head gleamed like the brass work on a navy ship, and was only equalled in

brilliance, by three gold teeth that were displayed prominent-
ly whenever he talked. However, all that was forgotten
when he smiled. Some men smile with their lips, and others
with their mouths but Clifton Riley smiled with every muscle in his face. And when he talked of God a sort of radi-
ance transformed his features to something soft and beautiful, until even the unsaved remarked to themselves, "Here
is a man who has known God."

*   *   *

Mrs. Morelin and Tom were alone at their barren homestead on Turkey Creek. The widow was standing beside
the pump, rubbing her hands on her apron and looking
out over the squalid little farm yard, and her son was busy
hoeing their patch of drouth-scorched corn.

"Tommy, I've told you time and again not to leave that
gate open so's Betsey can get in to the corn."

"Shut it yourself, if you want it shut," he said shortly.
"Cain't you see I'm busy?"

"If your Paw was alive he'd tan your hide for talking to
your Maw that way, that's what he'd do."

"Quit naggin' at me, Maw. That's all you do anymore,
is nag at me! I'm gettin' tired of it." He put down his hoe
and sauntered over to close the gate.

Tears that had faded her blue eyes began to flow once
more down the care-lined face. "Go on, talk to your old
Maw like she was a dog," her upper lip trembled. "That's
all I'm good for anymore. Just kick me around like I
wasn't nothing but a dog." She sat down in the doorway of
the little sod shanty, and wiped at her eyes with the corner
of her dirty gingham apron.

Tom snorted disdainfully, and went back to his hoeing
without even glancing her way. Neither of them saw Gus

Craig as he cantered into the yard on his big buckskin mare. He stopped in front of Mrs. Morelin.

"Howdy, ma'am," he grinned.

"What do you want?" she demanded surlily.

"I just came over to pay a social call, and to tell you that you're goin' to have a neighbor."

Tom came over and stared at him sullenly.

"What do you mean?" the widow asked, her voice showing the fear that was in her heart.

"One of my boys is proving up on that little piece just east of you. We was over and looked at it. It's mighty good land."

"I been feedin' my cow over there," Tom cut in belligerently.

"Well, you're not going to do it no more! We're puttin' up a fence, right through here!" His hand described an arc that bisected the Morelin farmyard between the house and barn. The house lay towards Craig's homestead.

"But you can't do that! This is our land!" Mrs. Morelin said, her pulse throbbing in her throat.

"Oh no it ain't! Your old man must've been likkered up when he built that house. It's clean over on our property. Anyone can see that."

"If you put up that fence," Tom gritted, his narrow face going ashen, *"I'll kill you!"*

Craig's beady eyes leaped upon the boy, and for an instant it seemed that he might run him down with his horse, or kick him in the mouth with a heavy boot.

"Tommy, boy!" his mother cried. "Go into the house."

"I ain't going to do it!" he retorted defiantly. "No danged cowpoke is goin' to scare me out!"

"Won't you go, Mr. Craig?" the widow pleaded. "We don't want no trouble. Please go away!" Her voice was coming in dry, strangling sobs.

"O.K. But don't forget," Craig called over his shoulder, "we're putting up that fence."

When he had gone Tom forgot that he was taking the place of a man, and sobbed in his mother's arms, sobbing tears of frustrated rage, mingled with terror.

"What are we goin' to do, Maw?"

"I don't know, I don't know," she repeated over and over in a sort of doggerel.

"I'll ride in and see the Parson," he announced, choking back his sobs and drying his eyes on a filthy sleeve. "He'll know what to do."

Fearfully his mother helped him catch up their old horse, kissed him, and watched him ride frantically towards town.

* * *

Martha, Mrs. Riley, and Nancy were chattering happily in the kitchen when John and Mr. Riley put on their coats and went outside.

"We'll go down to the general store first," John was saying. "I took the liberty of renting a room for you and Mrs. Riley."

"I'm glad you did, and I know Maw'll be pleased, too. I wouldn't know where to find a room in this here town. Do you reckon we ought to fetch our suitcases along now?"

"I don't hardly think so. It's a tol'able long walk, and we'll have to borrow Dozbaba's team, anyway, to make those country calls. We'd just as well wait till we get them to haul your baggage up town."

As they got to the gate, a lathered mount pounded up to them in a swirl of dust, and a youthful rider leaped to the ground.

"Oh, Parson!" Tom cried, his voice quivering. "I just got to talk to you!"

John noted that the boy's face was white, and dust had crusted the tears that streaked down either cheek. "What's the matter, Tommy?"

"I just got to talk to you, that's all." He looked at Mr. Riley distrustfully. "Can I see you alone, Parson?"

"Of course you can, Tom, but you don't have to worry about Brother Riley. Tell me, is there something wrong at home?"

"Plenty!" he blurted. "That — that blamed Craig!" He was struggling to keep back the tears. "That Craig's been pesterin' me and Maw again."

"What's happened? What did he do?" John asked anxiously, realizing only too well what Craig and his rough and wild cowhands were capable of doing.

In a tight voice Tom told him what had happened. "Me and Maw don't have no friends but you, Parson. We just don't know what to do."

Mr. Riley's eyes snapped. "Is there a lawyer here, Brother Woodring? I don't think that man can do what he says he's going to, if the house was built in good faith that it was on the rightful property. Tom's Paw didn't know he was building on somebody else's land. This Craig might make these folks pay something for that little chunk of land, but I don't see how he could chase them out of their own home."

They went to find the town lawyer, only to learn that Craig was entirely within his rights to force them out of their house; whether it was built knowingly, or unknowingly, on his land.

"It ain't right!" Tommy Morelin blurted. "Paw didn't do it on purpose, and Maw and me aren't hurting nothing.

It's only a little teeny corner of his land, anyway; and he couldn't use the house. He'd build clean down by the spring."

"I'm sorry, lad," Lawyer Nelson replied smugly. "The Parson here read the law to you right out of the book. There's nothing we can do. If Gus Craig's a mind to, he can put up that fence and drive you out of your house. Even if it was a frame building, you wouldn't be able to move it."

John nodded. "That's right, Tom. It don't seem honest, but it's the law." Nelson was one of Hart's men, the same as Craig, but there was no need in denying the truth. This time the law was on the rancher's side. "Come on, Tom, we'd better go out and talk with your mother. She's going to be worried to death about what's become of you."

They tied the boy's mount behind Dozbaba's buggy and drove rapidly towards the Morelin homestead.

"There's one thing that's in your favor," John remarked as they rode along the rough trail. "He'll have to get surveyors out to go over the lines again, and check them, before he does anything else. Maybe they'll find out that he's wrong."

"Them surveyors aren't goin' to go traipsing over our homestead, I'll tell 'em that," Tom vowed.

"But you'll have to let them. They got a right to survey and see who's right."

"We're right, and they won't set foot across the line as long as I got my rifle handy."

"Now Tommy," Mr. Riley said. "I'm not much of a one to be giving another man advice, but you couldn't do no good thataway. You'd only make things a lot worse than they are right now."

"They couldn't be."

"Oh yes, they could," John echoed. "You might hurt somebody, bad. You promise us that you'll let them surveyors alone. The way it is, the worst thing that could happen to you is having to build another soddy. I'll bet you'd have a deal of help doing it too. There's lots of sod, you know."

"Yeh, there's lots of sod, but there ain't lots of windows and doors and boards for the floor. Me and Maw can't buy none of them things. The only place we got is the haymow in the barn, and it ain't long till winter."

"We'll fix everything out, some way, I'll promise you that. Only I want you to promise me that you won't use your gun. Will you do that?"

"All right," he agreed reluctantly. "I probably wouldn't have done nothing anyhow."

"Will you let me borrow it for a few days? Just till things cool off a little."

"I would, Parson, only sometimes all me and Maw has to eat is some rabbits I kill, and a few spuds. I won't use it when the surveyors come, I promise."

"That's good enough for me."

At the homestead John and Mr. Riley tried to console the poor widow, but she was on the verge of hysterics and reasoning was of no avail. She refused to listen when he spoke of helping her. She had cried until the sobbing was scarcely audible, and the torrent of tears had been reduced to a trickle. Her eyes were red and swollen.

When the offer of their help failed to have an effect on her, John talked with her of Christ, of His matchless strength and help during times of trouble. He told her how Jesus had held him up when everything had looked the blackest. But all she could do was mumble somewhat incoherently.

"What kind of a God would turn all this trouble loose on a poor, defenseless widow? God's never done nothing for me. All I've ever had was trouble, and now me and Tommy baby is out in the cold."

When they tried to tell her that trouble wasn't meted out by God as a form of punishment, she kept on talking in that high-pitched monotone that verged on hysteria. After a time, however, they did succeed in quieting her a little. John wanted her to go into town with them, but she refused. Then he suggested sending one of the ladies out to stay with her, but that, too, was met with scorn.

Suddenly she turned on them. "I sent Tommy in to get you to help us, but you all side in with that Craig and his gang. You're one of them, that's what you are. I thought you'd help poor folks like us, but you're no better than the rest." She was violently angry now, and her voice crescendoed like a rising wind. "Get out of here, Parson!" she screeched. "And don't you never come back! We can get along without you and your kind!"

When they were out on the main travelled road, Mr. Riley said, "Don't worry about what she said, Brother Woodring. She was so hysterical and so bad scared that I don't reckon she hardly knew what she was saying."

"Things like that don't bother me much any more, since I come here," John replied, "but we got to help them, whether they want us to or not."

"It's going to be a hard thing to do, when both sides is against us. Maybe Craig was bluffing when he said what he did. You know a fellow like him might do that without ever planning on taking their house. It'd cause him a lot more trouble than it's worth. If we hear any more about it, we might be able to go out and talk him into trading that piece of land for another of about the same size. The man ought to be reasonable."

"Yeh, he ought to be reasonable, all right, but when you know him like I do you'll doubt it if he will be." They rumbled into town and down the wide, sandy main street. "Would you like to see where we'll meet tonight?"

"Sure would."

"It's not so nice as some places, by a heap. I know I had some buildings that was better, on my circuit, and they weren't much to talk about."

He turned up the side street and stopped in front of the building. For a moment he stared at it. There was a log chain across the door, with a heavy padlock sagging in the middle. The sign he had painted had been jerked down and thrown in the gutter. The windows were boarded.

"Something's happened," John exclaimed under his breath. "I'll bet Hart's behind this."

Chapter 11

THEY scoured Regina Springs for a place to meet. There weren't any buildings that were entirely satisfactory, but two of those they looked at could have served the purpose. One was a large, vacant blacksmith shop, and the other was an old livery barn. But they weren't for rent. Hart had seen to that.

"When I think of the way Hart's doing, I just feel like going out and knocking his teeth clean down his throat!" John raged.

"But that wouldn't do any good, Brother Woodring. I reckon I'll have to tell you like we told Tommy. You'd only make matters worse."

"I know, but it'd make me feel a whole lot better. You don't understand what it's been like, Brother Riley. I've been trying so hard to get a church started here and every single thing I've done, Hart's tried to block. A body can only stand so much!"

Mr. Riley turned the team in at Dozbaba's and stopped beside the barn. "Did you ever try winning *him* for the Church?"

"I tried to talk to him about spiritual things, but he wouldn't even listen."

"Then I think we'd best be praying for him, instead of wanting to fight him."

John burned under the indictment, for he realized that once more his temper had slipped away from him. He knew that he shouldn't become angry that way, and he tried not to, but at times it threatened to enslave him.

"I'm sorry I got temper-headed, Brother Riley," he said. "That's a fault I been strivin' to overcome for a long time."

Wisely Mr. Riley said nothing, and they walked along for a block or two. Every five or six steps he had to trot a little to keep up with John.

"Why don't we go talk to the man, Brother? Maybe the two of us could make him see how important it is that we have a place to meet tonight. Maybe we could get him to let us use it, just this once."

John shook his head. "It'd just be a waste of time. He's afraid of the gospel, and he hates me. That's why he's doing this. I know Julius Hart."

"Folks'll be coming in a couple of hours," Mr. Riley commented. "And some of them'll be from a long ways off. If we don't have a good meeting for them, we'll never be able to get them back."

"I know it. That's been worryin' me. But what are we going to do?"

"I reckon we could meet outside, if someone was to fetch a piano or organ to that vacant lot alongside your place."

"Say, that would work, wouldn't it?"

They went down to Cressland's lumber yard and rented two dozen planks to use as seats, and borrowed all the nail kegs that he had. At first he was reluctant to help, but after Mr. Riley talked with him a few minutes, he sent his man with a wagon to take the planks and nail kegs out to the vacant lot. They gathered old boxes and crates on which to put the rest of the planks, and Mr. Cressland made half a dozen low sawhorses to fill in.

They backed two wagons together in front of the seats, to serve as a platform, and strung a rope above the wagons, with six or eight lanterns suspended from it.

They were just hoisting Belle's organ up into one of the wagons when the first buggy stopped in front of the sod house. It's occupants, squatters from down on the creek bottom, had seen the church building locked and barred, and had driven down to John's to see what was the matter. Mr. Riley gave their twelve-year-old youngster a dime to stand in front of the building and direct folks to the meeting grounds.

"I reckon this'll do fine for tonight," John said when they were in the kitchen washing up. "But how'll we manage tomorrow evening, and the next, and the next? Folks'll sit out there and fight mosquitoes and bugs for one night or maybe two, and like it, if the entertainment's good. But they won't do it for very long."

"Don't you think there'd be a chance of finding some building to meet in?"

"Frankly, Brother Riley, I don't." He dried his hands on the roller towel and stepped into the other room. "We've got a few minutes before eight o'clock. Let's hold a short prayer service before we go."

They called the women into the room and, standing in a small circle, each offered a prayer for the meeting that was about to begin, and for a place to worship in the future.

"Oh Lord," Belle concluded in a hushed voice, "Bless and care for those who will bring the message tonight. Open the hearts of those who are listenin'; so that they might know Thy glories, as Thou hast so recently shown them to me. Help us to find a place to meet indoors, and help us to get a church organized real soon. In Jesus' Name we ask Thee, Amen."

The vacant lot was jammed that evening. All the seats were full, and men crowded in a sprawling semi-circle, five or six deep, about them. Rigs of all descriptions were lined up along the streets for two blocks in every direction. Ranchers and homesteaders, cowboys and hired hands, were jumbled together like beans in a sack. For the moment, at least, a truce had been declared.

Mr. Riley opened the meeting by singing a sweet old hymn, "The Old Rugged Cross." Belle accompanied him on the organ, and Nancy played her violin. To the simple plains people it sounded beautiful indeed, and a hush fell over the big crowd. John gave the evening prayer, and then Mr. Riley launched vigorously into the meeting.

"There's a lot of people here tonight. Folks that have come from a long ways off to be at this meeting. I don't know very many of you down there, and I reckon there aren't so many of you folks that knows all those sitting around you, either. So, as we sing this number, we're going to get acquainted with the fellow behind us.

"Do you all know the words to that old favorite, 'Bring Them In'? I'll sing it through for you first.

> " 'Hark! 'tis the Shepherd's voice I hear
> Out in the desert dark and drear.
> Calling the lambs who've gone astray,
> Far from the Shepherd's fold away.
>
> " 'Bring them in, Bring them in,
> Bring them in from the fields of sin!
> Bring them in, Bring them in,
> Bring the little ones to Jesus!

" 'Who'll go and help this Shepherd kind,
    Help Him the little lambs to find?
    Who'll bring the lost ones to the fold
    Where they'll be sheltered from the cold?'

"Now, everybody stand up and sing. I want you to really open up your mouths and let those words get out. And when we get to the chorus I'll tell you what to do!"

The little band of Christians in the wagons sang lustily. After a wavering beginning, the audience joined in until the place resounded with the song.

On the second chorus Mr. Riley lifted his voice and shouted, "Now when you get to that line, 'Bring them in from the fields of sin!' each one of you turn around and shake the hand of the person just behind you!"

When they tried it, and found the persons behind turned around too, a titter of giggling swept over the crowd, and swelled to a roar of laughter.

The rest of the meeting was a huge success. Nancy played her violin, and Mr. Riley sang several hymns, much to the delight of the listeners. Everyone joined in on the congregational singing. Few knew the words, but they followed those who did, or hummed along with the music.

Ranchers and homesteaders seemed to forget their differences, and several of them smiled and talked with each other as they filed out. John and Mr. Riley were very pleasantly surprised at the number who stopped to congratulate them, and say that they were going to be out for the meeting the following night.

When at last the lot was almost empty, Mr. Cressland, and Mr. Dozbaba, and two more of the town's leading citizens called John aside, just as they had done at a previous meeting when they told him that he must move or lose their support. This time their faces were different than they had been before, alight with happiness and enthusiasm.

"The meeting tonight was a humdinger, Parson," Mr. Cressland began eagerly. "I never did hear a man sing so good. I'll bet you get a whopping big crowd ever' night he's here."

"Thank you, Brother Cressland," John said reservedly.

"I owe you an apology, Parson. I can see now that you was right, and we was wrong."

John thrust out his hand and took Cressland's warmly. "I'm right glad you feel different about it. Having you men mad at me has been on my conscience for quite a spell. I'm terrible sorry I lost my temper that night when I tried to show you my way of thinkin'."

The lumber man accepted his apology, and then went on, "We're behind you one hundred percent. After the meeting tonight we're sure that you and Rev. Riley are just the men to start us a church. We want to help what we can."

"That's fine," John said. "We're going to need all the help we can get if we're going to get any place at all with it."

"We know all about Hart renting that building so it couldn't be used for a church no more. It's a sin and shame, that's what it is."

O'Connel nodded his agreement with the lumber man.

"We don't want to interfere with your plans, Parson, but we figured as how we ought to have a place where we could meet inside. The bugs is pretty bad this time of year, and if it'd rain, the night's service would be ruined."

"We reckoned that, Brother Cressland, but there isn't a place in town that we can get. Just before we come over here tonight, we held a prayer meetin' about that very thing."

"That's right, maybe," Dozbaba put in, "maybe we can rent nothing in Regina Springs too, but there's more than one way of skinning a cat than twisting his tail. Down by Omaha is a man what's got tents; big tents, little tents, all kinds of tents."

"We want to rent a tabernacle to hold the meetings in," Mr. Cressland continued. "Two or three weeks of meetings like these ought to give us enough people to start thinkin' about building us a church of our own."

"God bless you, men," John said, his voice charged with emotion. He shook hands with each of them.

"The Lord has answered our prayers almost before we asked of Him," Mr. Riley observed.

That night was one of rejoicing at the Parson's. Jim Hart came over, and Nancy shyly introduced him to her parents. Martha put a jar of cookies and a cake on the table, and Belle made the coffee for the impromptu party. It was after two when they finally said goodnight, and went to bed.

Chapter 12

THE enthusiasm kindled that night flamed to new heights in the meetings that followed. Any place that John chanced to go around Regina Springs, he could hear men and women talking about the meetings. Some were for them, and others against, but very few remained indifferent. On three successive nights Mr. Cressland sent down additional planks for seats, and still the number standing continued to grow. The story spread that they were soon to have a tent in which to meet, and already men were talking of building a church. Homesteaders and ranchers began nodding to each other when they met on the street; and, while the greetings were far from cordial, the fact that they spoke at all indicated that the barrier was being lowered. It seemed, at last, that God had blessed the work at Regina Springs, and it was about to burst into full fruit.

After supper, on one of the few free evenings that they had, John and Mr. Riley were sitting alone in the parlor. Nancy was out riding with Jim, and Martha and Mrs. Riley were in the kitchen clearing up the dishes.

"I've been thinking, Brother Woodring," Mr. Riley said, leaning his bald head back against the chair and fumbling with his watch chain. "The big trouble between the nesters and ranchers isn't land, and it's not very often that it's grass. There's still plenty of both, and I don't reckon there'll be enough homesteaders come in here to do a whole lot of bothering on that score. This's cow country, and always will be."

"That sounds reasonable to me, but what keeps them at each other's throats like a pack of starved wolves?"

"Neither bunch'll even try to see the other fellow's side. The cattleman won't think about nothing but cows, and the farmer won't think about nothing but crops. Because they don't understand each other, they hate, and are scared."

"I don't quite get what you're driving at, Brother Riley."

"Well, put it this way. A homesteader comes out here and stakes out a claim. Naturally, if there's water around, he files on the land joining it, if he can. He don't even think about the fact that some rancher might've been watering his herd at that spring or creek for five or ten years, and there's not another water-hole close by. The farmer plants corn down along the water, and the first thing you know the cowman's herd tramples it. The squatter gets mad, and up goes a fence. Maybe the rancher, or his cowboys lose their tempers and jerk it down. Any way it happens, you got what it takes to make plenty of trouble."

"I'd never thought about it that way."

"You and I, Brother Woodring, are the only ones that can do much of anything about it. I think both sides trust us. If we were just able to get them together to work out their difficulties, everything'd be peaceful here. Why, I reckon most of these cases wouldn't only take a little giving in on each side. All we got to do is make them see that there's water enough for everybody; and that the rancher's got just as much right to water his cattle as the homesteader's got to protect his crops, or vice versa."

"I think you're right, Brother Riley!" John exclaimed. "Here I been studying and praying about some way to get them together, and you think of it right off the bat."

The next morning they set out together. The plans were made to hold a joint meeting of the ranchers and homesteaders after the services on the following Monday night. The tent was scheduled to arrive on the local Friday, and the two ministers expected a record turnout, for that was to be the first night they'd hold services in the new tabernacle. No better time for the proposed conference could have been found. And, as soon as this matter was disposed of, the way would be cleared for a concerted drive to organize the church congregation.

The response from both groups was guarded; but they indicated that they'd be willing to try it, if the others would. John and Mr. Riley purposely left Craig till the last, so that they might come to him with the assurance that every other interested party had agreed to attend the meeting, and try to cooperate in making a settlement.

When Mr. Riley finished talking to the Box Bar Y owner, Craig lifted his voice and shouted, "I ain't havin' nothing to do with you or any plans you got! Get out of here, before I set the dogs on you!"

John's temper seethed and bubbled, just beneath the surface. "We want to talk to you about Mrs. Morelin and Tom, too," he said, managing to keep the anger-bred tremor from his voice. "Isn't there some deal we could make with you so's those poor folks wouldn't lose their home?"

"The only deal I'll make with them is for 'em to move, pronto. And, by grab, they're goin' to move as soon as I can get some surveyors out from North Platte to check those boundary lines again. If them fellows hadn't been so busy this month, I'd have that trash off my land by now!"

John would have said more, but Mr. Riley sensed that talking with the man was useless, and drove away. "You can't reason with a man when the devil's putting words on his tongue, Brother Woodring."

"No, but I reckon there's one way we can take care of him. That house don't mean nothing to Craig and Hart. It's just pure cussedness that's making them act that way. We'll get a bunch of the folks together and build the Morelins a house. We'd ought to be able to get the wood fixtures they'll need, too. There's plenty of sod, and we can get all the help we need."

"That had ought to be a fine way to take care of it. Craig might get mad, but there's nothing much he could do."

The tent came, and by Monday evening the crew of volunteers had it up and ready for the meeting. Across the front they had built a low platform with a pulpit to one side, and two rows of seats for the choir along the back. A series of lanterns were strung about the tabernacle, and the song books were lying, at regular intervals, on the seats.

John was right about the crowd. By seven-thirty, they filled the seats and spilled over into the aisles until they bulged the tent. The canvas sides were rolled up and tied, and the late-comers stood around on the outside, looking in. Hart and Craig, and one or two of their cowhands were sitting up towards the front. Perhaps they had changed their minds and had decided to cooperate. At any rate Mr. Riley and John would have the chance to talk with them.

When the first chord of the opening hymn sounded, half a dozen rough, boisterous young cowboys jostled their way down to the very front row. Hart's son, Roy, was at their head. Children were sitting on the plank, but the boys forced themselves in, squeezing the youngsters together like oranges in a crate, until some scooted off the opposite end of the seat. John rose to speak to them, but the choir had already begun to sing, and those who had been forced from the plank were sitting comfortably on the ground.

Then the newcomers began to clap and stomp their feet. Belle played louder on the piano, and the choir sang a little louder, but they were drowned out by the noise. John held his hands in the air. The music stopped, and the boys sat back, smirking.

"I'm going to ask you young men to do one of two things," he said loudly. "You must either be quiet or leave."

The music had no sooner started, and the congregation had begun to sing, when the clapping and stomping began again. John could feel the color rise in his face. Martha must have seen it too, for she leaned over and whispered, "Be careful, dear."

He stepped deliberately off the platform, and with one motion, grabbed young Hart by the ear and hauled him to his feet. John was smaller than he by half a head, and his hands would have enveloped the Parson's like a catcher's mitt holds a fielder's glove. Nevertheless John marched Roy outside.

"I asked you to be quiet or leave," he said. "If you ever come back, just remember that!"

The rest of the party left also, cursing and threatening.

As John got back to the pulpit, Julius Hart, Craig, and the others in their group got to their feet noisily. "I reckon us ranchers ain't wanted here!" Hart rasped. "Come on, fellows! We don't have to be *asked* to leave. We know when we're not wanted!" They stomped out in single file.

There was a rustle over the crowd, a murmur like a sudden gust of wind, and a shuffle of feet. One by one the cowmen followed Hart's leadership and went outside. A few remained, but there weren't enough of them to even hold the meeting between the ranchers and homesteaders. John sat in his chair, too astonished and stunned to say a word to stop them.

Somehow the ministers got through the service, but it was very disappointing. John's preaching was dull, as though his mind were far away, and Mr. Riley's singing was listless and very ordinary. There was no happy, excited conversation when the service was over. No one crowded about the pulpit, as they had done before, to ask about future plans. The meeting that should have been the best was by far the worst. John had the desolate feeling of failure, as they filed outside. Mr. Riley patted him comfortingly on the shoulder, and Jim Hart took him by the hand.

"I'm right sorry for the part Paw and Roy had in that affair tonight. They'll have to settle with me for that!"

"Now, Jim, I don't reckon that'd help any. It'd probably just make them madder than ever at all of us."

"All right, Parson, but just remember, I'm with you!"

Back in their bedroom that evening John and Martha talked long after everyone else had gone to bed.

"What's the matter, honey? That wasn't my fault tonight. Yet I kind of got the idea that everyone blamed me. Some of them ranchers that walked out with Hart has been coming to meetings right along. And I thought we were making a lot of progress with them. Why did they follow him? Has he got such a hold on them as all that?"

"I reckon maybe a lot of them does as he says, but I think they were disappointed in you, John dear," she replied candidly. "Because you lost your temper."

"The only thing I thought about was getting them young hoodlums outside," he flared. "Most anyone would've done the same thing."

"Yes," she said softly, "there's a lot of truth in that, but they judge you and me and the Rileys by a different code than they use for themselves. Their own kind can get temper-headed, and make public exhibitions, and they don't think nothing about it; but they expect Christians to be *different*. We've got a big responsibility in belonging to the family of God."

He dropped heavily to the bed and combed his fingers through his hair. "I've tried to fight it, Martha, but it's no use. The harder I try, the madder I get."

She came over and sat down beside him. "Do you take it to the Lord, John, and ask His help?"

He shook his head. "I reckon this is one thing I got to fight out alone."

"Have you forgotten what Jesus tells us? '*Whatsoever ye shall ask the Father in my name, He will give it you.*' I've been praying for you for a long spell. Why don't you add your prayers to mine tonight?"

For the space of a minute he stared at her. "I don't know why I ever reckoned I'd ought to fight it myself, but it seemed like I shouldn't ask God for help doing something I should be able to do myself."

"But you see now what happens when we try to rely on ourselves alone.

"You're right, Martha." He smiled weakly. "I reckon you're always right."

Together they knelt and prayed.

Chapter 13

JIM HART spent every spare moment with Nancy that she would allow him. They went walking and riding together, or sat in the parlor with John and Martha, playing dominoes, and talking endlessly.

Jim brought a wiry little gray mare to town from the Box Bar Y on the pretext of getting her shod, and quartered her at the livery barn. She was the pick of the ranch's riding stock; as gentle as an old shepherd dog, and as fast as most race horses. Nancy grew to love her easy, rolling gait, as they rode on long, moonlight canters over the prairie. Under Jim's tutoring she became as proficient in the saddle as a man, and they dashed headlong over the sandhills, across ground riddled by prairie dog holes, and wide blowouts that threatened to spill their mounts at every step.

Occasionally she fixed a picnic lunch, which they would eat beside some scraggling willows or jack pine that had defied the wind and heat and drouth, to grow beside the creek. On these excursions they took either Martha or Belle along, but still folks spoke of it with their tongues in their cheeks. The stories spread. It was rumored that she didn't even use a side saddle!

John knew that all the talk was idle gossip, but it worried him, for he realized what damage just such idle gossip could cause, both to Nancy's reputation, and to his own efforts to build a church. Jim's every action was labeled with sincerity, and yet the Parson couldn't help wondering. Every other person connected with Jim's father was bitter in their denunciation of the church, and had labored hard to prevent its success. Could it be that he was using Nancy for some, yet undisclosed, plan to make trouble?

Several times John had broached the subject of Jim's accepting Christ as his Personal Saviour, but the big cowboy wasn't responsive at all. He either switched the conversation, or bluntly told John that he wasn't interested.

"That Bible stuff's all right for women and kids, and maybe for guys like you, Parson," he said on one occasion. "But it ain't for the likes of me. Why, the devil'd feel like he was insulted right personal, if I wasn't sent down to shovel coal for him."

"You shouldn't say such things, Brother Hart. You're joking about something that hadn't ought to be taken as a joke. I'm real serious when I tell you that I'm worried about you." He intended to add that he was worried for Nancy too, but Jim cut him off sharply.

"Don't you worry about me none, Parson. I'm not worth it!" he lashed. "And don't call me Brother Hart."

John and Martha prayed continually that the cowboy's heart and eyes might be opened, for Nancy's sake as well as his own. John thought probably that she was praying for him, too.

Something seemed to have gone wrong with the revival meetings. Mr. Riley's singing was just as good, John's sermons were just as stirring, and the crowds were almost as large as ever, but their enthusiasm was gone. They first noted the lack of interest in the free will offering and choir row. Both began to dwindle.

Night after night the two ministers pleaded for the repentant souls to come forward and give themselves to the Master. Men who were smiling pleasantly during the singing suddenly froze at the first semblance of a call for sinners. Their eyes hardened and their bewhiskered lips clamped resolutely shut, as though they were daring John and Mr. Riley to convert them. They had come to be entertained, and nothing more.

The way things had been going there was no chance to even talk about organizing a congregation at the present. The month passed as quickly as a January thaw, and it was time for a complete report on their progress.

It was no surprise to any of them when they received a letter from the district superintendent in answer to their report, stating that the Bishop felt that work in Regina Springs should be indefinitely suspended. He enclosed the Bishop's letter by way of explanation. John read it aloud.

"'. . . I do not doubt that Brother Woodring and Brother Riley have expended every effort to establish a church in Regina Springs, and I do not want this move to reflect, in any way, upon their ability or sincerity. I have the utmost faith in both of them.

"'If our funds were unlimited, I would be only too happy to have them continue indefinitely. As it is, however, we must so steward our money that it will accomplish the most good, and reach the largest number of people . . .'"

Mr. Riley shook his head, his usually jovial face clouding. "I hate to have to go, Brother Woodring," he said. "I reckon we haven't been making so much progress, but I never doubted at all that we'd be able to get a church going after awhile."

"But you *can't* leave!" Belle protested fearfully. "What could we do without you?"

John saw more behind her statement than regret over seeing them go. There was fear that she'd be unable to maintain her faith alone against the blandishments of her associates; and fear for Clara, whose life was still steeped in sin.

"I don't want to leave, Sister Williams," John replied sorrowfully. "I reckon I want to stay until we get this town cleaned out, and a fine church going strong. I want that more than most anything I ever wanted in my life."

Martha went over behind his chair and slipped her arm about his neck. "I'm not so sure that we ought to go away from here till we get things started like you want them, John," she said.

"But we'll have to do what the Bishop says, darling. We couldn't stay on here without the support of the Church. What would we do for victuals, and rent and clothes? How'd we live?"

"The apostles didn't have anyone giving them a check every month to pay their expenses, but they didn't quit. They kept right at their work till they finished what they set out to do."

"I reckon they did, but —," his voice faltered, and he looked at her again. "You aren't really serious, are you, Martha? I mean it's one thing to have faith, and a different thing entirely to throw ourselves on the mercy of these people. Why, they'd let us starve!"

"Maybe they would, but God wouldn't." Her brown eyes were snapping. "You've been preaching about faith ever since we came here. Let's show them what faith'll do."

"But what about the church authorities?" Mr. Riley protested. "You know we're both under the supervision of the superintendent and the Bishop. They might have some other place where they think we could do more good."

"How could we possibly do more good than we can right here?" Martha asked. "I'm reckoning Bishop King'd give us leave to carry on, and his prayers with it. Why, he said in his letter that the lack of money was the only reason he's moving us, and giving up this town. He wants a church here as bad as we do, and I'll wager he's spent more than one sleepless night thinking about this place."

John stroked his chin thoughtfully. The question was too big to be decided on the moment, and yet there was no other way. If they should decide to remain in Regina Springs, they would have to get a letter down to North Platte the next morning in order to catch the mail train to Omaha.

"It's most time for the meeting over at the tabernacle," he said at last, looking at his watch. "Let's all come back here afterwards and pray this thing through. Whatever we do, we want to be on solid ground, and to know that it's God's will."

As Nancy sat down in the soprano section of the choir, her blue eyes caught Jim's unruly pile of hair, thrust half a head above those sitting on either side of him. He looked awkward and ill at ease in a new blue serge suit that fit him a bit too snugly across the shoulders, and a bit too loose about the waist. He was wearing a white shirt that made his sun-browned face look even darker than it was. It was surprising that he had come to church; for always before he had hung around outside, waiting to take her home. She colored as her eyes met his, and she bent over her song book hastily. A broad grin enveloped his features.

When the meeting was over he came to the front and asked to take her home.

"I reckon I could go home with you," she agreed.

"What's the matter, don't you want to?"

"It isn't that, silly, but I've got to go right home tonight. You see, we're holding a sort of special prayer meeting at the house."

"What's the trouble, didn't you get enough praying done for one night?"

"John's got an awful hard thing to decide." Briefly she told him what had happened.

"You don't mean to tell me that you really expect praying to help any?" he asked, incredulously.

"Of course we do." The complete assurance and finality in her voice silenced him momentarily.

"You're folks'll leave anyway, won't they?" he said as they neared the house.

She nodded.

"What'll you do then?"

"I reckon I'll help John and Martha if they decide to stay. My violin playing might help a little with the meetings."

"I sure do hope you stay."

"So do I," she whispered softly.

"Do you have to go in?" he asked.

"Yes."

"I sure wish you didn't. Can't you just skip this meetin'?" he insisted.

She shook her head. "I'm sorry, Jim, but I reckon not."

"Well then, do you care if I come in and hang around till it's over?"

"Why, of course not," she said. "We'll be happy to have you."

The rest of the group were sitting solemnly about the small parlor when they entered. Mr. and Mrs. Dozbaba, and the Cresslands were there, along with Belle, the Rileys, and Martha and John. Without speaking Mr. Riley brought two chairs in from the kitchen.

John got to his feet and said, "I reckon you all know why we're holding this prayer meeting tonight. We've got to decide whether or not to step out on the faith that God will provide for us, and stay here in Regina Springs. We've met to petition the Lord for guidance."

Mr. Riley quoted a passage from the book of Psalms, and Nancy read a portion of Acts. Then they all bowed in silence. After a moment or two John spoke quietly. "May we have a few volunteer prayers?"

"Oh Heavenly Father," Belle began, after a slight hesitation. "I don't know much about prayin' before anybody, but I do know how bad we need a church in Regina Springs. I guess maybe I feel different about this than some, but, you see, I wouldn't have known Christ at all if it hadn't been for the Parson. I got lots of friends here in town. Mostly they're bad clean through, but there aren't any of them worse than I was. I want them to have a chance to know Jesus, too. So, if it fits into Your plans, dear God, please let the Parson and Martha stay. In Jesus' name we ask Thee, Amen."

"Our Father who art in heaven," Mrs. Riley prayed. "Give these young people Thy wisdom in making this choice today. Guide them and watch over them, and counsel them carefully. If it's Thy will that they stay here, please give them the courage to carry through. In Jesus' name, Amen."

There was a slight pause when they came to Jim. "You can count me out," he muttered uncomfortably when he realized that they were waiting for him, "I never prayed in my life."

"Our Heavenly Father," John concluded. "Guide us now as we seek Thy will. In Jesus' name, Amen."

There were half a dozen audible sighs as they lifted their heads.

"Jim," the Parson ventured, his voice still hushed. "Would you please get that Bible on the table behind you?"

The cowboy turned around and picked up a book beside the lamp. "Is this it?"

"No, it's the other one. That's a dictionary."

"Oh, I see that now." He started to hand it to John, but he waved it aside.

"Just open it to some bit of the Scripture and read, won't you please?"

"What is this, a joke?" The question went unanswered, for his eyes caught Nancy's, and the message that he saw there was as plain as though she had spoken. She was asking him to do as the Parson wished. Grimly he opened the Bible, leafed through a few pages uncertainly, and said, "Does it make any difference where?"

John shook his head.

Jim's face flushed, and he began to read, stammering and stumbling over the words like a first-grade boy reading before his class. " '*Which-of-you-by-taking-thought-can-add-one-cubit-to-his-stature?*' " The little group was electrified, as Jim's words hammered into their minds. " '*And - why - take - ye - thought - of - raiment? Consider - the - lilies - of - the - field, - how - they - grow; they - toil - not, - neither - do - they - spin: - and - yet - I - say - unto - you, - That - even - Solomon - in - all - his - glory - was - not - arrayed - like - one - of - these.*

" '*Wherefore - if - God - so - clothe - the - grass - of - the field, - which - today - is, - and - tomorrow - is - cast - into - the - oven, - shall - He - not - much - more - clothe - you, - oh - ye - of - little - faith?*

" '*Therefore - take - no - thought - saying, - What - shall we - eat? - or - What - shall - we - drink? - or - Wherewithall shall - we - be - clothed?*' "

They sat in astonished silence, as though they might have been struck dumb by the very nearness of God. For several long minutes conversation was suspended, and even their breathing seemed subdued, while the Spirit filled their hearts.

John got to his knees before them all and thanked Him for showing the way. His voice was hushed, and charged with emotion. Martha was as radiant as she was the day that they were married; and Belle, who sat next to her squeezed her hand happily.

There was no merriment at all in the quiet conversation that followed, as there usually had been on previous nights at the Parson's home. Those who spoke at all, spoke softly and reverently, as they would in some beautiful church. Even Jim seemed affected by the meeting. When the guests began to leave he sauntered out onto the porch with Nancy to say goodby to them. John and Martha went out, too, but as soon as the last couple disappeared into the darkness they went back inside, leaving Jim and Nancy alone.

"Wasn't that meeting marvelous? I never did feel so close to God."

"I don't know, it gave me the willies."

"Oh Jim, I'd just give anything if you was to accept Jesus."

"Now listen," he retorted roughly. "I came out here to talk with you, not to be preached at."

Nancy did not reply.

"If it wasn't so late," he said, changing the subject, "I'd sure like to go for a ride. I been looking forward to a long ride with you, alone."

Her eyes were dreamy, and her thoughts rambling. "Why alone?" she asked innocently.

"So's I could . . ." he gulped hard, and took a step towards her. "So's I could kiss you!" With that he took her in his arms and pressed his lips fiercely against hers. To his surprise she clung to him. "I never thought I'd ever say this to any woman, Nancy, but I love you."

She freed herself slowly, and turned away.

"Do you love me?"

There was no answer.

Gently he turned her around. "Do you love me?" he repeated.

"Yes, Jim," she said frankly. "I do love you. That's what makes it so hard."

He was so flustered that he didn't notice her last remark. He fished around in his pocket and got out a small square box. "This ain't much, but it's a diamond, and the best I could afford to buy. I wish it was a heap bigger."

She looked at it; and, when her eyes lifted, there were tears in them. "It's beautiful, Jim darling. It's about the most beautiful ring I ever saw. But I reckon I just can't take it, or the vows that go with it."

"And why not?"

"You aren't Christian, Jim. That's what I been trying to tell you. I couldn't marry anyone who wasn't a Christian."

"So that means more to you than I do!"

The tears were spilling from her eyes, and she dabbed at them with a dainty handkerchief. "Yes, it does. It means more to me than anything else in the world."

"All right," he retorted angrily. "I'll be a Christian, then."

"That won't do, Jim. You don't just be a Christian, like you join a lodge. When you come to Christ, you've got to come for Him alone, not for me, or anyone else. Don't you understand?" she pleaded.

"No, I don't!"

"I'm awful sorry." She laid her hand on his arm.

"I'll bet you are!" He jerked away and strode off the porch.

Nancy watched him until he was out of sight, then went into her room, and threw herself on the bed, sobbing.

Chapter 14

THE next morning John took his arm out of the sling. It was a bit weak, but it seemed good to be able to use it again. He and Martha drove the Rileys to North Platte, from where they were going to their new assignment. At the last minute, Nancy decided against riding along, and kissed her parents goodby at the house before they left. She excused herself by saying that there wouldn't be room for five in the buggy without crowding, but her tired, haggard eyes and strained face bespoke another reason.

"I'm tol'able worried about Nancy," Mrs. Riley said, as they drove along. "She looked awful peaked to me this morning."

John would have spoken, but Martha cast him a quick, forbidding glance.

"I'm worried about her, too, but it's not her health that's bothering me," Mr. Riley answered, clucking to the team.

The chill fall wind gave way to the caress of a pleasant September sun, and the long ride passed quickly. It was shortly after noon when they pulled in to North Platte.

"God bless you, lad," Mr. Riley said before the young couple left them. "I only wish we were staying with you. But you know, the Lord's work has got to be done, and we've got to go where we're sent. I'm right positive that you can succeed alone, as well as the two of us could have. We'll be praying for you constantly."

"Thank you, Brother Riley. We'll be needing all the help we can get. And we're going to miss you a heap."

On the way home Martha told John what had happened between Nancy and Jim.

"I've been afraid something like that was about to break," he said. "Jim's a good boy, but he's set his heart so strong against the Lord that I don't believe no man can change him. There ain't no use of my saying any more to him. He flies back at me like a tabby cat with her first litter of kittens."

In the days that followed Martha was so exuberant and hopeful for the future that John almost forgot his misgivings. After considerable thought and prayer they decided upon holding only the mid-week prayer meetings and Sunday Services, putting aside the nightly revivals for the present.

At first, conditions warranted optimism. Cressland and Dozbaba had given voice to the Parson and his wife's plan to remain in Regina Springs on the faith that God would provide for them, and a thankful people showered them with gifts. Each family gave what they could, and it wasn't long until their pantry was stocked with home canned vegetables, and meat, and jellies. There were five hundred pounds of potatoes in the shallow cellar to the left of the house, and one homesteader brought in half a hog when he butchered. It was dressed, and cut up, ready to be put down in brine.

Everything was going along so splendidly that it already seemed that their faith had been richly rewarded. John was looking forward to the time, in the not too distant future, when he might be able to kindle enough enthusiasm, in enough people, to build a church.

About a week after the Rileys left he got a letter from the Superintendent expressing his deep gratitude for keeping the field open in spite of a shortage of funds. And the next day they received a splendid letter from the Bishop personally, commending them highly for their faith and courage, and assuring them that support would be renewed at the earliest possible moment.

The letters were very encouraging, but the subsequent events proved that the young couple's optimism was premature. John completely lost touch with the ranchers. He had been branded as a partner with the homesteaders on the night of that unfortunate affair in the tabernacle, and they treated him as one of them. As long as the Rileys remained, a few cowmen had hung on just to hear Mr. Riley sing, but now that he was gone, even those refused to come.

A case or two of violence broke out between the ranchers and homesteaders, and the flames of fury were fanned high. There were fights whenever they chanced to meet, and one luckless farm hand was mobbed and beaten up terribly after tangling with a cowboy. The law enforcement officers were either powerless or indifferent, because they made no effort to interfere.

Both sides blamed the Parson for the trouble. The squatters charged that he deserted them in attempt to effect peace, and the ranchers claimed that he incited the homesteaders to fight.

Church attendance tumbled, until only two or three rows of seats would be filled on Sunday morning. Enthusiasm that had been so high, ebbed away into indifference, and John's own hopes crumbled with it. The old doubts that he had fought for so long came cropping back into his thinking, like bindweed that grows again after being hoed out each summer and fall. There were doubts that God had intended for him to go into the ministry, doubts that they should have stayed in Regina Springs, and doubts that they would have enough to eat, and enough clothes to wear throughout the winter.

A month had passed, and still Jim didn't come around to see Nancy. She tried to carry on as though nothing had happened, but the ache in her heart persisted in popping up at unexpected times and making her miserable. Usually she and Martha confided in each other about everything, but there was a strange reluctance to talk this over with anyone. If she could only see him, that would be enough. Whenever the hoof beats of a galloping horse sounded along the street, she flew to the window and looked out, hoping to catch a glimpse of the wiry little buckskin that belonged to Jim. At times, when it was likely that he might be in town, she found some excuse to go to the general store on Main Street, but she never encountered him. One evening she casually mentioned him to John, and the Parson remarked that he hadn't seen Jim since her folks left. That night she cried herself to sleep.

It was about this time that Martha began to sew and plan for the baby that she was so sure was resting just beneath her heart. Nancy was elated when she told her, and immediately started making little flannel kimonos and long, lace-fringed dresses. Men may bicker, and quarrel, and fight, but to women, a baby is a baby, no matter who his mother or father might be. The wives of some of John's most bitter enemies slipped away to the Parson's house while their husbands were in the saloons. They brought baby clothes and quilts with a never ending stream of advice.

Ordinarily John would have been as greatly pleased as any man awaiting his first born child, but under the circumstances it filled his heart with dread. There would have to be a doctor consulted frequently, and Martha would need plenty of fruit and milk, and good, nourishing food. She would need rest, and sunshine, and freedom from worry. He had seen too many twisted, malformed babes and semi-invalided mothers in the Ozarks, all because they couldn't afford, or were too ignorant, to take proper care.

It was bad enough for him and Nancy to face hunger, but for Martha, now, it might be fatal. He spent long, tortuous hours on his knees with no definite assurance or answer, while things continued to get more and more unbearable in the dirty little town. He almost grew to hate the place.

Martha brushed aside his fears with a smile. Her faith was as unshaken as a mighty redwood tree amidst a storm, and she went serenely ahead with her plans.

It had been several weeks since Hart had said or done a thing, and John found himself growing restless and uneasy.

"It's not like him, Martha," he said, as they were walking home from the tabernacle one Sunday evening after a particularly dull service. "I don't know why, but I'm kind of worried. I feel like something's going on that we don't know nothing about."

"You should ought to be happy that nothing has happened, dear. Maybe he's had a change of heart."

"Not that man. A fellow might kill him, but you'd never change him."

Martha looked up abruptly. "John, did you leave a light burning in our parlor?"

"Why no," he answered. "There must be somebody there."

They quickened their pace. "Maybe it's Nancy," Martha panted. "She walked home with one of Dozbaba's little girls this evening."

"It couldn't be them, they're still behind us."

The pale, yellow glow was going from one room to another, wavering and moving about, as though the person holding it were searching for something.

John sprinted on ahead and flung open the door. There was Belle, with a lamp in her hand, standing in the middle of the parlor floor, amid a broken heap of dishes and pictures and books. The house looked like a bar room that John had seen before he was converted, after a rough and tumble fight. The table and chairs had been splintered in hammering great chunks of plaster off the walls with them. The horse hair sofa had been ripped open with a knife, and the stuffing strewn about the floor.

"I heard them, Parson," Belle faltered. "But I was afraid to come over till they left. They was all drunk, and it was awful!"

John stepped through the rubble to peer into their bedroom. It had received the same treatment as the parlor and kitchen, and not a thing was spared. Their only clothes that weren't destroyed were those which they were wearing.

He heard a weak little scream and ran back into the parlor. Martha had crumpled in the middle of the room, sobbing pitifully. Belle was already kneeling on the floor, her strong, capable arms cradling the younger woman's head. "There now, honey, this isn't helping none."

John squatted beside her, his own sinking despair engulfed in pity for her. "Let's not cry any more, darling," he said tenderly. "Everything'll turn out all right. There wasn't a thing ruined that can't be bought again."

"I know," she answered in a strained voice, that was struggling against the tears. "But I been working so hard to m-make it pretty," she choked. "And now it's all gone." One hand aimlessly lifted a shred of lace. When she saw that it had been torn from the little dress which Nancy finished only that afternoon, her sobbing burst out anew.

"We'd better take her over to my house," Belle suggested. "That bunch of drunken hoodlums are prob'ly still in the gambling room, but we can slip upstairs without lettin' them see us."

Together they got her to her feet, and half carried her across the dusty street to the boarding house. Nancy came along just as they were going up onto the steps and John called to her. She helped Belle and John get Martha upstairs to one of the empty bed rooms and in bed. Belle brewed a steaming pot of tea, and after Martha drank it she felt a little better.

The party downstairs was reaching uproarious heights. Thick, guttural laughter and the clink of glasses were punctuated with a high pitched, piercing shrill that became more and more frequent as the evening wore on.

"That's Clara," Belle told John, when they were out in the hall. "She's always drank a lot, but yesterday afternoon she and Craig and Hart started on a drunken spree. They're the ones that got the men to go over and ruin your place last night. Parson, I been praying' about Clara ever' night since I found Christ, but she just won't listen." Her voice was weighted with sorrow. "I don't know what to do."

"You've tried pleading with her, so have I, and we've both been praying for her. She's got to take the next step herself. We can't force her to become a Christian."

The noise downstairs crescendoed to new levels as the hours passed. At three o'clock Clara lurched into the kitchen and fried a couple of eggs and made some coffee for Craig and Hart. She was weaving unsteadily, and leaned against the table for support. Suddenly her face blanched, and her eyes were glassy. She staggered towards the door, but halfway there began vomiting blood. Hart and Craig got hold of her, and between them, they carried her to the parlor couch. It sobered both of them; and, when Julius Hart went to the stairway to call for Belle, his voice was steady. Craig ran to get the doctor whose home was four blocks away.

John came downstairs too, and sat on the couch beside the stricken woman; while Belle stood anxiously to one side. Once more he pleaded with her to accept Jesus as her Personal Saviour. She was conscious, but still defiant.

"You're in a bad way, you know that, don't you, Clara?"

"I'll come out of this all right, Parson. I've come out of them before," she gritted.

" 'All we like sheep have gone astray; we have turned every one to his own way: and the Lord hath laid on Him the iniquity of us all.' "

"What does that mean in our language?"

"I can answer that best with another portion of the Scriptures. In Romans Paul said, 'For all have sinned and come short of the glory of God.' Like I told Belle, we've all sinned so much that there isn't much difference between any of us. Christ has taken those sins, or will take them, if we'll only let Him. 'Behold the Lamb of God, which taketh away the sins of the world.' "

"He can have mine," she gasped roughly.

The doctor came in just then, and John stepped aside. Clara's breath was coming in short, quick jerks and her eyes were becoming set and staring. He took one look at her and shook his head.

"What-chance-have-I-got, Doc?" she managed to ask. "I-want-the-truth."

"I know you, Clara, so I'm going to tell you the truth. I've warned you about this b'fore," he said brutally. "I told you what would happen if you kept on drinking. Now it has happened, and there's nothing you, or me, or anyone else can do."

For the first time fear flashed into her eyes, and terror transformed her face.

"Parson!" she cried in terror, raising up on one elbow. "Parson! What must I—? How can I—?" Her head dropped lifelessly to the pillow. The doctor felt her pulse, and slowly pulled the covers over her head.

Belle was standing as though she were carved from wood. Her face was expressionless, and her eyes were fixed on some distant spot.

"I've been tellin' her all the time that she'd ought to see the Truth and accept Christ. But she wouldn't listen. *She wouldn't listen!*" Belle collapsed into John's arms.

*　*　*

After the funeral Belle asked John to help her, and they carried all the gambling equipment out into the alley and burned it.

"I want you and Martha and Nancy to stay here with me, Parson," she said. "I'm cleaning out that trash that's been livin' here. If you folks can get along on faith, so can I."

Chapter 15

THE next few weeks were the most difficult that John had ever spent. There were four of them now, and if it hadn't been for a few good neighbors who were sorry for Belle, and brought in food, they would have gone hungry part of the time.

"I don't know what to do," he said one evening while they were still at the supper table. "We're facing a right serious situation. The past two Sundays there hasn't been hardly anyone out to church. We aren't gettin' ahead at all."

"It's beginnin' to look that way." Belle's simple black dress of mourning made her eyes look sunken and very tired. They were veined with red, as though she had been crying a great deal when no one was about. Her voice was tinged with discouragement. "Maybe there just isn't supposed to be no church here," she said.

"Sometimes I'm wondering that myself. I was so sure that God would take care of us, but all we've had is trouble."

Nancy, who hadn't spoken before, looked up. "But John," she said. "I don't think we've given the Lord a chance. We've only allowed Him a few weeks, and we've had plenty to eat. He's seen to that."

"I'm thinking about the future, Nancy," he replied. "Belle's the only one of us that's got clothes for winter; and I've got Martha to worry about, and the baby. We just can't get by this way no longer."

"Don't you remember the Scripture that Jim read?" Martha asked. "That was a definite answer to prayer, and I'm as positive as I am that we're sitting here, that we'll get along all right, and get a church formed, too."

"I wish I shared your optimism, darling."

Before the women had finished the dishes, Mr. Cressland came to call. He and the men who were renting the tabernacle were becoming disheartened. The expense was becoming burdensome, and it didn't seem to them that there'd ever be a church until more homesteaders moved in. Finally John talked them into giving him fifteen days more in which to produce results.

This was the church's last opportunity in Regina Springs for a long time, he knew that. If he failed, then the children who were playing in the streets today, were doomed to evil and sin tomorrow. With his failure written against the town, other denominations would hesitate to come in, and it might be years before the Word of God would be preached here again.

The only hope was in bringing the fight with Hart right out in the open, John decided. With a series of nightly meetings, he planned on launching an attack against vice that would rock the town; and end, either in his complete success, or in his being driven out of Regina Springs.

The next day two new boarders appeared at the Williams Boarding House and took rooms. One was a wandering printer who planned on starting a newspaper, and the other was a hardware dealer who was placing great hopes in the area's becoming a homesteaders' paradise. The latter had already shipped his stock in from the east. They paid their rent in advance, and Belle served the little group meat for the first time since they moved in with her.

* * *

Jim Hart let his buckskin gelding pick the gait, and they swung along at an easy, comfortable walk. He was hunched in the saddle, with his hands folded over the horn, his bony knees cocked high, and his hat pulled down to shade his eyes. His usually clean-shaven face bristled with reddish brown whiskers, and the hair at the nape of his neck curled upwards from his shirt collar.

For the past several weeks he'd been riding aimlessly about the Box Bar Y range, checking herds and gathering strays. The routine matters he attended to, but his work had suddenly lost its savour. There was a time when he had sought the company of others, but now he cared only to be alone. He wanted time to think things through. Ever since that night at the Parson's, Nancy and the prayer meeting had been seared into his heart with the branding iron of love. For some reason the two were inseparable, one calling to mind the other.

At night he dreamed of her, pleading with outstretched arms for him to come with her to find Jesus; then that picture faded, and in its place appeared the spectre of Clara, who had waited too long. When he awoke, the chill ball of ice that lay, unmelting, in the pit of his stomach, had grown larger than before.

There was something different about Nancy, and the Parson and his wife. At first he thought that it was because they had more pleasing personalities than folks around Regina Springs. They carried an air of serenity and happiness that no one else seemed to possess. But it couldn't be personality, because Belle had acquired the same qualities upon becoming Christian.

The prayer meeting, itself, was disturbing. They hadn't prayed as he thought of prayer, with fancy words and high sounding phrases. Rather, they talked with the Lord as one person to another, as friend to friend. There was no doubt in any of their voices that He could and would, help them. The sudden, obvious answer to their prayers was what bothered him the most. Of course it could have been coincidence, his chancing upon that particular portion of the Scriptures that so aptly fit their situation, but it didn't seem likely. If anyone else in the group had read it, he'd have sworn that it had been planned ahead. But he couldn't have done so, even if he'd wanted to, because it was the first time that he could remember having a Bible in his hands. Back at the ranch house that night the battle within him raged with a seemingly increased fury, as he strove to reach a decision.

The others had already eaten and gone back to the bunkhouse, or off to town, when he came into the kitchen. Beulah, the old colored cook, who had been with his father ever since he could remember, was busy at the dish pan, singing a happy, lilting spiritual.

"Swing low, sweet chariot, comin' for to carry me home,

Swing low, sweet chariot, comin' for to carry me home."

"Why, hello there, Jimmy boy. I never heerd you come in."

"I come in on my tiptoes, Beulah."

"Aw, git along with you," she scolded, " 'fore I take the coal shovel to you."

He sat down beside the big coal range and crossed his legs. "What's the chance of gettin' anything to eat around here?"

She bustled over to the stove, shook it, and put in a stick of kindling. "You know you c'n have somethin' to eat, no matter how late you comes in."

"Wasn't that a spiritual you was just singin' when I come in?" he asked.

"Uh-huh, some times the Lord just takes hold of my heart and how the song rolls out!"

After a time he said, "Tell me, Beulah, how did you get to be a Christian?"

She looked at him, a bit startled.

"What's the matter? Are you surprised to hear me askin' that?"

"I shore am!" she exclaimed. "I never did hear you say anything about the Lord, before."

"Well, I'm kind of surprised at myself."

"It sounds mighty good to your old Beulah's ears, Jimmy boy. Your Mammy was a fine Christian lady, I tell you." She sat down in a chair beside the table, and continued. "It was a long time ago, that I become Christian, but I remembers it like I does yesterday. I was down by the river one day a-listenin' to a revival meetin' when the preacher comes over to me an' says, 'Sister, the devil's got your name writ down in his book an' his old mouth's jist a-waterin' for you. While there's time you better let the Lord take them sins away!' So I got down on my knees, prayin', and the Lord done set me free. I'se been thankin' the Good Lord ever since. You don't know what glory it is!"

Jim could scarcely remember his mother, she had died when he was so young, but somehow it made him feel good to hear that *she* was Christian. Perhaps the whole family would have been different if she had lived. Suddenly, without any advance warning, the storm within him subsided. His heart accepted, without question, that Christ was his Saviour, and he longed for Him.

"This baptizin'," he said hoarsely, "Do you have to be baptized to be Christian?"

"Just let me study a little." She sat there a moment, her black brow wrinkled in thought. "Seems as how baptizin' has somethin' to do with it, but I remembers some folks down south who 'got religion,' and there wasn't no preacher anywhere's around. They never got baptized for six months. So I reckons maybe you kin be a Christian without bein' baptized first."

"I want to be a Christian," he said simply.

"Does you believe that Jesus come to take your sins away?"

He nodded. "Yes, I do."

"Does you accept Him with your heart, an' want to follow Him?"

"Yes."

"Does you aim to follow Him no matter what happens, or what bad things the devil puts in your way?"

"Yes."

"Has you prayed for Him to take such a miserable sinner, and make you clean?"

Instead of answering Jim slipped from his chair to his knees, praying. His prayer was silent, torn, word by word, from his contrite heart. He knew nothing about praying or prayers, but he understood the blackness of his life, and the overwhelming desire to have it wiped away. He also understood the peace that came over him as he knelt there. It was deeper and more real than anything he had ever known before. His whole outlook on life changed at that instant. And he found that life, itself, took on new meaning to him. Now, he understood how Nancy could refuse to marry him, in spite of her love.

He got to his feet, a trifle embarrassed, and started outside.

"I reckon you is a Christian, now, Jimmy boy. I can see it in your face."

He did feel different; clean and fresh inside, like the smell of new cut hay, or a breeze after a spring shower.

Beulah got a Bible from her room and handed it to him. "This Book was your Mammy's once, Jimmy. She asked me to save it for one of her boys, but I wasn't going to give it to you less'n you'd appreciate it."

She told him something about the Bible, and helped him find some portions of the New Testament that she thought he should read. When he went back to the bunkhouse some two hours later he took the Bible with him.

Early the next morning he left the ranch, and rode directly to his father's saloon. When he told Julius that he had become a Christian, the older man flew into a rage.

"No son of mine's goin' around prayin' and bowin' and singin' like an addle-pated fool!"

Jim tried to reason with him, but it only increased the fury of the tirade.

"If you walk out that door before you say it ain't true," Julius blustered, threateningly, "I'll disown you! You won't be no son of mine."

Jim looked at him, sorrowfully. "I'm right sorry you feel that way, Paw," he replied. With that he turned on his heel.

He went back to the ranch and packed his clothes. For the present, at least, he decided against saying anything to Nancy or the Parson. It would be better to have a little time to his credit, to show her that he hadn't become a Christian just to win her hand.

In the days that followed he filed on a homestead along the creek, bought a few head of stock, and set about building a house. With every stroke of the hammer he dreamed of the day when he and Nancy would live there, together.

Chapter 16

JOHN announced the nightly meetings in the tabernacle on Sunday evening, and opened with a bitter attack on Julius Hart and the things he stood for. Not many in the congregation agreed with him, and those few who did were afraid to say so; but they were all back on Monday night to see what would happen next. The crowds leaped to capacity at the meetings which followed.

At first the saloon crowd laughed it off. One of their number, who had undoubtedly had something of a formal education, referred to him as the 'Don Quixote' of the sandhills, and the name caught on. Soon all of his enemies were calling him by that name. When they learned that Jim Hart had deserted their number and become Christian, they were more angry with John than they'd ever been before. Julius Hart increased the rounds of free drinks and talked darkly of what they'd ought to do to "that Parson."

Being men who lived by impulse, they were ready, after the first drinks were downed, to go after him and ride him out of town on a rail. This time they vowed that they were going to *finish* the Parson for good, and drive him back where he belonged. While Hart awaited the proper moment to send them into action he fanned the mob's hatred, as a blacksmith pumps the bellows on a forge, until it flamed white hot. Men were muttering on the streets, and the saloons were filled with fighting talk.

The story of Jim's conversion came to John in Dozbaba's General Store. At first he didn't quite believe it, but when he learned that the young cowboy had been disowned by his father, and had filed a claim on a homestead, he knew that it must be true.

There would be one person even more eager to learn of it than he had been. As soon as he could get away, he hurried back to the boarding house and found Nancy. She was alone in the kitchen, ironing.

"I heard something uptown today," he began, "that I reckon you had ought to know."

"What's that?" she asked disinterestedly, without looking up.

"It came from a tol'able good source, and I'm positive that it's true." He looked at her, but she was absorbed in her own thoughts, and was scarcely listening. "Jim has accepted Christ."

"What?" She dropped the iron, and her face paled.

"It's true, Nancy. He became a Christian and his own Paw won't have anything to do with him because of it. He's took out a homestead out on the creek, and is living out there by himself."

She sank weakly into a chair close by, tears brimming in her eyes. "Thank God," she breathed reverently, her face aglow. And, as he looked at her, John almost felt like crying too.

*　　*　　*

Tom Morelin and his mother had been up since dawn, moving their few belongings from their sod house to the barn. Its leaky roof and ill-fitting windows hadn't made it much of a house, and the widow had complained bitterly about it; but it had kept out the cold, and it seemed that they were losing their most priceless possession.

Craig had been over with his surveyors the day before, rechecked the boundary, and gave them until eight in the morning to get their furniture moved out and across the line. It was half past eight now, and everything was gone, except the bed in one corner of the kitchen where Tom had slept. A pair of old boots and a tattered jacket were lying on the floor close by, where he had thrown them.

"Come on, Tom," Mrs. Morelin urged. "They'll be ridin' out here any minute, and if we don't have these things over to the barn like as not they won't let us have them."

Her eyes became watery again, and Tom looked at her scornfully. "Quit your bawlin', Maw," he ordered, with the impatience of youth. "I'd just like to see one o' them come nosing around here. I'd just like to see them! We ought to stay, that's what we ought to do. Me an' Paw built this house, and it's ourn."

Nevertheless Tom lifted the mattress obediently, and was about to take it outside when Craig rode up on his big blaze-faced roan. He was alone.

"Oh, here he is now!" Mrs. Morelin cried.

"Let me talk to him!" Tom growled. "Just let *me* talk to him!"

"You got to get out of here, Tom," Mrs. Morelin gasped. "You got to hide."

"I'm not hidin' from no blasted cowpoke."

"Do as I say," she said authoritatively. "There's no tellin' what he'll do to you."

"I'm not goin' to hide," but his voice was tinged with the fear that was so prominent in hers. All at once he became a little boy again.

"Get under the bed," she said. "I—I'll talk to him, then there won't be no trouble."

"I told you to have this junk out of here this mornin'!" Craig blustered as he threw open the door. "Did you think I was foolin'?"

"W-w-we was just gettin' our things out," she apologized, stepping backwards. "It won't take us much longer. All there is left is this here bed."

"I got a mind to throw you out!" Craig advanced menacingly. His breath was loaded with alcohol, and he was spoiling for a fight.

Under the bed, Tom was terrified. His breath was coming in quick, dry gasps that shook his frail body. His right hand went out slowly and felt something cold and hard and round. His fingers curled around it and he drew it close to him. It was his .22 rifle that had fallen down behind the bed.

"I said, I got a mind to throw you out!" Craig snarled. He pulled his gun out of its holster. "Now beat it, before I use this thing!"

Mrs. Morelin screamed.

Tom shoved the bed aside, jumped to his feet and shot without realizing what he was doing. A blank look came over Craig's face. He swayed slowly, trying to speak, but the words only formed on his lips. His knees buckled, and he slumped to the floor. There was a small, black hole in his chest.

"Oh Tommy! Tommy! Tommy!" Mrs. Morelin cried, gathering the frightened boy in her arms and holding him close. "What have you done?"

Tom was sobbing too.

After a few minutes Mrs. Morelin harnessed the horse, and they drove at break-neck speed in to Regina Springs to the only friend they knew, Parson John.

As soon as John saw them pull up in front of the house he knew that something was wrong. The widow was sitting very straight, her eyes staring forward, and her whitened face an expressionless, immobile mask. Tom was huddled lifelessly beside her, his head muffled into his coat, and his arms hanging loosely at his sides. At first John thought that the boy had been injured, and he dashed out to the buggy.

"What's the matter?" he asked excitedly.

Neither of them answered, and John took hold of Tom's shoulder. "What's the matter?" he repeated.

"Tom—just—killed—Gus—Craig," the widow mouthed in a dull monotone.

The answer startled John. He felt the color drain from his face, and his heart-beat quickened.

"How did it happen?" he managed to ask.

As she told him, Tom began to sob again, his narrow shoulders quivering with grief and fear. John climbed into the buggy beside him, and put his arm comfortingly about him.

"There now, Tom. Everything's going to be all right." The boy quieted a little, and the Parson said softly to Mrs. Morelin, "We'd better fetch him down to the marshal."

"Oh, no!" she protested. All of her equanimity vanished, and she, too, began to cry. "We can't do that! He's one of Hart's men, and he'll let them take Tom! They'll *hang* him!"

"He'll get a fair trial, Sister Morelin," John reassured her. "That's the only way. Believe me."

"But they won't never let him come to trial. I know these men! They've just been waitin' for a chance like this. They'll go down to the jail and get him! Then they'll drive all of us homesteaders out'n the country!"

"You let me take him to jail, and I'll give you my word of honor that Tom'll be safe from harm. From what you said I'm tol'able sure that no jury'd convict him. But we've got to obey the law, don't you see?"

Reluctantly she agreed. The Parson drove Tom to the jail at the far end of main street. After talking with the marshal he called North Platte, reporting the murder, and the sheriff said that he'd come out with the coroner as quickly as possible. Then John took Mrs. Morelin back to the boarding house with him.

The news spread about town like a prairie fire driven before a high wind. When Hart heard it in his 'Gold Eagle Saloon' he poured himself a big drink, downed it in one gulp, and dashed the glass to the floor.

"Everyone that's ridin' with me, come on!" he grated, striding through the bat-wing doors. A score of men followed him, their anger rumbling like a live volcano that was stirring restlessly.

They rode out to the Box Bar Y, increasing in numbers as they went. Every ranch along the trail had its volunteers. At the fork that turned off the Morelin's homestead Hart halted them.

"A couple of you guys go over and stay with Craig's body. Them sneakin', thievin' squatters is liable to try getting it away so's the sheriff wouldn't have no evidence on the kid!" he shouted. "The rest of you come on, and we'll get the hands at my ranch, then we'll be ready for action."

"What we goin' to do, J. C.?"

"We're going to clean out every last one of them blasted squatters like we'd ought to done a long time ago. Then we'll go back to town and take care of the kid and the Parson!"

"That Parson's the guy that's behind all of this!"

"We'd never ought to have let him get off the train here at all! We've had trouble ever since he come!"

"Maybe we'll string him up beside the Morelin brat! He's the one what put 'em up to fightin' us!"

A hoarse shout of approval went up. In their present mood, that mob of men were capable of anything.

"We'll burn out the other nesters, all right, but what about Jim?" one of the riders asked.

"He's one of them now."

"And he ain't no better'n the rest. I say give it to him like we do the others!"

Julius Hart paused, as though he hadn't thought of his own son. The men grew restive, eyeing him speculatively, and a wave of muttering swept over them.

"By grab!" Julius cursed. "We'll burn him out, too!"

Another shout rent the silence.

Fortunately Jim wasn't at home when the men rode up. His house was of sod so they couldn't burn it, but they knocked in the windows, battered down the doors, and set fire to the little furniture that he owned. Julius Hart lit the first match, and ignited a pile of dry hay under the table and chairs that were piled together in the center of the room. They completely gutted the buildings, set fire to a hay stack Jim had just bought and hauled in for the winter, and killed his four cows.

By that time the men were thirsting for blood, and decided upon riding directly to town to lynch young Morelin, and take care of the Parson.

Old Dozbaba saw the cloud of dust on the hills towards Jim's homestead, and surmised who the men were, and their mission. He hurried to tell John.

"Away we got to get that boy, Parson," he blurted. "They come after him, a whole cloud of them. By the talk uptown I hear what is doing, maybe. We got to get him away."

John put on his coat and stepped out into the waning afternoon sunlight. Something would have to be done. He could never let them lynch Tom. But how could he save him? The marshal wouldn't release Tom to him and the old storekeeper. John was as sure of that as he was that the fellow was one of Hart's henchmen, and would be eager to let the mob take Tom and do what they willed with him.

He got into the buggy with Dozbaba and they whipped the team to a headlong, spine-jolting run that hurtled the light buggy over the sand.

"Let me out at the jail," John said. "Then you drive as fast as you can out to the Morelin place. The sheriff's likely to be out there checking things over."

"And you, Parson?" the Bohemian asked. "You will be doing what?"

"I don't rightly know," he said truthfully. "But I'll try doing somethin' to hold them off."

John prayed silently, and more earnestly than he'd ever prayed before, that Tom might be saved. In some way, somehow, he had to handle this mob of men who hated him.

The jail was a squat little two-room building, made of heavy lumber. Half of it formed the marshal's quarters, and had an ordinary frame door, while the other room was a barred and padlocked cell. It was made for drunks and minor offenders and was never intended to hold anyone who might want to get away. Whether the marshal was inside or not, John didn't know, and he didn't have time to find out.

As the men came thundering up the street, he picked up an oak singletree from the ground nearby, and implanted himself firmly on the steps to the building's only outside door.

They slid to a stop in front of him, and the dust billowed for just a moment, hiding their faces. As it settled back to the street, he recognized many of them. They were men he'd seen about town quite often. Some had been coming to church regularly before the Rileys left. They had seemed like honest, forthright citizens, but now their faces were distorted with rage, the kind of rage that makes men kill.

Tom guessed what they had come for, and was screaming hysterically. He was like a young panther caged for the first time.

"We've come for Morelin, Parson," Julius Hart announced, stepping forward.

"This ain't the way, Brother Hart," John replied in a loud, clear voice that carried above the babble of the men. "Why don't you let the law take care of this? That's the only way!"

"That's not our way! We take care of things like this, personal! Step aside!"

"You'll only make matters worse! He'll get a fair trial, and if he's guilty he'll be convicted."

"He's guilty all right!"

"He's just a boy, Julius. Think of your own sons."

"I only got *one* son, thanks to you, Parson. After we take care o' the kid, we're fixin' to take care of you!"

"What you do to me don't matter so much, 'cause I'm a grown man, but let the law take its course with this boy. I'm not saying he did right. That's for the court to decide, but you want to remember that Craig was threatening his mother. That alone ought to entitle him to a trial."

"It'll entitle him to nothin' but the short end of a lariat rope. That's what it'll entitle him to."

"If you hang this child you'll be sorry of it all the rest of your lives!"

"Let us worry about that. Now, you either get down from there and clean out of the way, or we'll come up there after you!"

"I'm ready!" John defied them, swinging the singletree like a baseball bat. "You might get me, but I'll bet I take care of a couple of you first!" The old fire gleamed in his eyes. His hat had fallen to the ground, and his red hair was tousled. He looked like some medieval peasant about to club a wild boar.

The door behind him opened and the marshal thrust out his head. "What's the trouble, Boss?"

"Get that fool Parson out of the way, Bailey!" Julius Hart ordered.

"Stick 'em up!" An electric shock pulsated up and down John's spine, as he felt the hard, round end of a forty-five revolver in the middle of his back.

But he spoke softly, without so much as shifting a muscle. "Go ahead and shoot, Bailey. That's the only way you'll get me to move."

There was a cold, metallic click of the gun hammer.

"Get out of the way, Parson!" The voice was slow and ominous.

"Go on, Bailey. You aren't afraid to shoot a grown man in cold blood, are you? You hadn't ought to be, because you're fixing to help hang a boy. What's the matter? What's bothering you?"

A hush had settled over the crowd, until only their heavy breathing was audible. The marshal's gun hand was trembling. "I said for you to get out of the way!"

"And I told you to shoot!"

"Drop that gun, Bailey!" A rasping voice blasted the silence.

Every eye turned, and with a lightning thrust, Jim Hart knocked the revolver from the startled marshal's hand. Bailey made a move for it, but Jim froze him in his tracks.

"If you go for that gun I'll crack your skull wide open with this two-by-four!" He added grimly, "Now get over there with the rest of them, where's I can watch you!"

The crowd was stunned temporarily by Jim's sudden appearance. He must have slipped around the side of the building while everyone was so tensely watching the Parson and Bailey.

As they began to find voice Jim continued. "You're a bunch of drunken bums, even if you are led by my own Paw. I know you was out to my place this afternoon and burned me out! But that don't matter. What I'm here for is to help the Parson keep you men from doin' somethin' you'll regret all your natural born lives. You've got to lick me and the Parson both, before you touch that poor defenseless boy in there."

They were still clamouring for action, like a man-eating tiger with the smell of blood in her nostrils. They crowded and shoved close about the little jail.

Julius Hart was standing silently. He had disclaimed Jim as his son, had even burned all the boy's possessions and killed his stock, but in spite of himself, he couldn't let that mob storm the jail with Jim standing in the doorway.

"Come on!" he shouted to the men. "What do we care who hangs him as long as he's hanged. Let's let the law do the hangin' for us!"

They shoved him roughly out of the way, and surged forward like floodwater bursting a dam. Julius shouted to them as he did of old, ordering and bullying, and cursing. But they were completely out of control, like animals lusting for blood.

At the moment Jim Hart and John expected the mob to rush them, a lathered bronco came thundering up the street, and slid to a stop. The lean, dust-plastered rider leaped from his mount and pushed through the angered men to Julius Hart. The roar of the crowd hushed, and every head spun to stare at the white-faced newcomer.

"Get a doc, J. C." he panted. "When I got out there to the Morelin place Craig wasn't dead!"

"What?"

The silence was deafening.

"I tell you Craig ain't dead! Leastwise he wasn't when I left! We got to get a doc, pronto!"

The mob froze as though they were petrified. A faint muttering went up, but it died suddenly.

"Come on down to the Golden Eagle!" Hart shouted, "I'm settin' 'em up!"

The rabble melted.

"Thanks, Paw," Jim said, offering his hand to his father as the others left.

"You ain't no son of mine!"

Chapter 17

WHEN the last of the mob disappeared into the saloons and the two young men were standing alone, John turned to the tall cowboy beside him. "Thanks, Jim," he said. "I reckon I would have been in a tough spot if you hadn't come along when you did."

Jim flushed self-consciously. "I was glad to be able to do somethin' for you. It wasn't much." He leaned against the corner of the doorsill. "Tell me, Parson, what'd you think about when Bailey shoved that revolver in your back?"

John looked at him, then laughed shortly. "It's a funny thing. I just remember that I was wondering if he'd really shoot."

There was silence for a few moments, then Jim said, "Well, Parson. I decided the grass was greener on your side of the fence."

"Yes?" As though he didn't quite understand.

"I done a lot of thinkin' out there on the range alone. I finally decided that you was right, and I was wrong. I'm a Christian now."

"I'm right glad you got fetched around to God's way of thinking. To tell you the truth, I'd heard it b'fore, but it's good to have you tell me. You won't find the way easy."

"I already found that out, Parson," he grinned wanly. "Paw and that bunch of drunken hoodlums burned my place out today. Everything I own is gone, except my saddle, and horse, and these clothes I'm wearing."

The Parson eyed him closely. "Are you sorry, Jim? Has
it been worth the cost of breaking with your Paw, and losing
all your friends?"

"*I found Jesus!*" he said simply. "There ain't no cost too
great to pay for that."

"Nancy was so happy when I told her that I'd heard you
had accepted Christ as your Saviour."

Jim's face brightened noticeably. "I been goin' to come
up, Parson, but I didn't want her an' Martha an' you to
think that I — that I took Christ just to win her. I wanted
to sort of make myself a reputation before I asked her again
to marry me."

"I reckon you really made yourself that reputation tonight." John brushed off his hat, straightened out the dents
as best he could, and put it on. "I think I'll just stay close
till the sheriff from North Platte takes Tom down there with
him. I don't hardly reckon them men'll come back, but
they might."

"I don't think they'll bother Tom no more," Jim replied.
"I'll tell you what. You got a meetin' tonight. Why don't
you go home and eat, and let me stay here to watch him.
I'll take good care of him."

"Thanks, Jim, I do need a few minutes to sort of get
hold of myself."

"Watch out tonight, Parson. That mob's all likkered up
and wantin' a fight. They won't do nothing to me, and they
can't do nothing to Tom, so you're the one that'll prob'ly
be the goat."

"I don't think they'd hurt me," John said, but his heart
refused to believe the words that he spoke so courageously.
Standing up to them had shaken him, and now he was
frightened at the thought of facing them again.

"Don't fool yourself. Look what they tried to do to Tom, and we were just lucky to have been able to stop it." Jim Hart took hold of John's arm earnestly. "Why don't you call off this meetin' tonight, Parson? When they sober up they'll have all the fire taken out of them. There'll be lots more nights that you can hold meetin's, and you won't be taking any risk."

It was a great temptation to follow Jim's suggestion and cancel the evening meeting, but he felt that if he obeyed, it would be the last opportunity that he'd have of forming a church. People won't follow a cowardly leader on a moral crusade.

"No, Jim," he answered. "It's not my will this time, but God's. I've got to trust that He'll take care of me."

"I knowed when I said that that you'd be sticking it out," he said admiringly. "Well, I'll be up front in the tabernacle, so's I can help a little if they try any funny stuff."

"I was in hopes you'd be coming over to the house before the meeting to see Nancy."

"I - I'll be over to the tent, soon as the sheriff gets here," he said. "If you don't mind, Parson, I'd sort of like to talk to her alone first."

John smiled understandingly.

As he stepped onto the porch of the boarding house, Mrs. Morelin ran to the door and cried tearfully, "How's Tommy? Is he all right? Is he safe?"

"Yes, Sister Morelin," he replied gently. "He's safe, and I *know* that he'll be well taken care of."

He told them nothing of what happened at the jail, except that he met Jim, and the cowboy was coming to the tabernacle if he could make it.

The tent was jammed to capacity when John and the women entered just before eight o'clock. He succeeded in

talking Mrs. Morelin into going along, and she walked beside Belle, a haggard, dejected figure. Nancy was dressed
in her prettiest frock. Her blue eyes were soft and haunt-
ingly beautiful as she searched the crowd for Jim. He was
sitting on the front row, flanked by youngsters whose heads
scarcely came to the points of his elbows, and feeling very
conspicuous. Nancy smiled at him, and he blushed to the
uppermost tips of his ears.

There were others in the tabernacle whom John wasn't
so glad to see. Julius Hart and twelve or fifteen of his
henchmen were sitting together in the center, and sprinkled
through the crowd, and he caught glimpses of some whom
he had recognized in the mob at the jail.

John felt hopelessly inadequate for the task at hand, and
his soul cried to God for help. The first hymn was finished
without interruption; and, if it hadn't been for the sneer-
ing grin on Julius Hart's face, his fears would have been
somewhat allayed.

They sang a second hymn and Nancy got up to play a
violin solo. John looked about for his sermon notes. In the
excitement he had left them over at Belle's on the dining
room table.

He leaned over to Martha. "Would you go and get my
sermon notes, darling?"

"Of course," she smiled.

The violin music was fast, and had a light, catchy rhythm.
There was a slight noise at the back of the tabernacle, and
Hart's men began to guffaw. Six boisterous young couples
were dancing down the aisle. Jim's younger brother Roy,
with a gun swinging on his hip, was in the lead. The others
were close behind. Julius Hart jumped to the plank seat
and began clapping his hands and shouting. His followers

did likewise until the music could scarcely be heard. The homesteaders cringed in their seats.

Nancy stopped playing, looked about hesitatingly, and then began again. Jim stepped up onto the platform beside her. The couples were right down in front when the Parson got to his feet, and, with a prayer unspoken on his lips, signalled for Nancy to stop playing.

"Lord, forgive them!" he shouted above the tumult. "For they know not what they do!"

Everything stopped, and for the moment all was silent. Then the couples who were dancing, broke and ran for the entrance. Hart and his men drew their guns and began to shoot. One bullet crashed into a lantern that was swinging from the top of the tabernacle, and it thudded to the ground. A stray shot zinged past John's shoulder and into the piano behind him. The main body of the congregation scurried outside, like quail seeking cover, or huddled between the seats. The mob, a score and a half strong advanced towards John. He stood there rigidly as though he were riveted to the platform.

"Now we'll take care o' *you*, Parson!" They were cursing violently.

"Bring in that bucket of tar and them feathers!" Julius Hart bawled drunkenly. "This time we'll get rid of the Parson pronto!"

Jim would have interfered, but they thrust him aside and grasped the Parson. John made no effort to resist. It would have done no good, for they'd have overpowered him in a moment.

There was a rataplan of hoofs outside, and a sharp, agonizing scream. And somebody yelled for the Parson. John tore away from the men who were holding him, and dashed outside.

There Martha was lying, in a twisted heap on the ground. "Martha!" he cried, throwing himself down beside her. "Martha! Speak to me!"

Belle kneeled on the other side, and lifted her head. "She's breathing, Parson."

"What happened?" His voice was dead and lifeless.

"Roy Hart's horse ran her down," Mr. Cressland said angrily. "I tried to grab her, but I was too late."

"Will somebody help me get her inside?"

Jim and another cowboy carried her into the tent. Somebody shoved three of the plank seats together, and they laid her on them.

"Someone's gone for the doc, Parson," Jim said.

"Thank you."

Julius and his followers were standing uneasily on the fringe of the crowd. They were reluctant to leave before learning how badly she was injured, but lacked the courage to stand with the others.

John had covered Martha with his coat, and was kneeling beside her, holding her limp, white hand in his own. A prayer surged upwards from his heart vaguely inarticulate, but like a mighty, swirling river in depth and intensity. She could not die, she *would* not. He looked over at Julius Hart, who was standing alone in one corner of the tent. It was impossible to read the emotion in his face.

The thunder of hoofs blasted the tense silence of the tabernacle, and a horse with two riders came pounding around the tent. The rider behind was holding the other youngster on.

"Mr. Hart!" he shouted. "Roy's horse stepped into a gopher hole and throwed him! He's bad hurt!"

Eager hands took the limp, bleeding lad from the saddle, and carried him in where Martha was lying. He groaned a little, and moved one hand slightly as they laid him down.

The doctor was working with Martha now, his capable hands moving mechanically. She hadn't stirred since the horse trampled her, and the only sign of life was the slow, regular heaving of her breast.

"Will she live, doctor?" John's lips formed the words.

"I can't tell you, my boy. We've one thing in our favor. The Good Lord takes care of these 'mothers-to-be' by giving them a stronger heart, stronger lungs, and a stronger constitution, than at any other time. If she isn't injured internally she has an excellent chance."

John knew what the old medic referred to for he'd seen women in the Ozarks lose their babies by miscarriage, simply by working too hard. And sometimes they lost their lives as well. There's no telling what such a jolt as the one she had taken might do. The anguish in his heart was reflected in his face. She *had* to get well.

In spite of his own fear he stepped over to the place where Julius was kneeling beside his son, and put his hand on the big man's shoulder. Strangely enough, for the first time since he'd been in Regina Springs he felt no fear or dislike for Hart. Julius was just an over-wrought father at the bedside of his boy.

"Can I do anything, Brother Hart?"

Julius looked up quickly, his eyes moist. "Would—would you *pray* for him, Parson?"

Without a word John got to his knees.

A short time later Martha regained consciousness, and called for him. John went over to her, and the doctor turned to his other patient, to make a more thorough examination.

Julius got up nervously and walked over to Jim and Nancy who were standing apart from the rest of the excited crowd.

"I want to apologize to you, Jim," the older man said bluntly, and loud enough for those standing close by to hear. "I been hatin' myself ever since you left, but I was just too blamed proud to call you back."

Jim took his father's hand happily.

"And I want to apologize to you, too, Miss. You're a mighty fine girl, and I want to wish you and Jim a lot of happiness."

They both blushed at that. Nancy, very discreetly, excused herself, and left Jim and Julius alone.

"Beulah was tellin' me that Maw was a Christian," Jim began after an awkward silence.

Julius nodded. "Your mother was the finest woman that ever lived."

"Were you a Christian, too?" he persisted.

"I don't know, son," Julius replied truthfully. "I guess I never paid much attention to that. Your Maw was always readin' the Bible and such. I kind of figured she had enough religion for the both of us."

"But she didn't have. I don't know a whole lot about it yet, but I found out already that it's something personal. You got to have it for yourself. All Maw could do for you is what I've been doin', that's *praying*."

"Do you mean to tell me that you've been prayin' for me, even after I told everyone that you weren't my son no more?"

"Yeh," Jim said. "You see, Paw, God is a God of love. An' besides, it don't make no matter what you did, or what I

did, you're still my Paw. Look what the Parson just done.
Roy ran down his wife, and she might be dying over there,
but he didn't get mad and rave, he came over and prayed
that Roy would get well. That's what bein' a Christian is
like!"

Julius walked outside, and Jim followed him.

"Paw," he said softly. "Why don't you quit fightin' God,
like I did. Why don't you accept Jesus?"

He could feel his father's gaze boring through him in the
semi-darkness. "Show me the way, lad," he said in a queerly
strained voice. "Show me the way."

Jim didn't know many Bible verses, and he didn't know
much about how to save souls, but he got to his knees and
prayed with his father that he might become One with
Christ.

Julius Hart prayed the prayer of the Publican, " 'God, be
merciful unto me, a sinner.' "

After a minute he turned to Jim and said, "But how do
I *know* whether I'm Christian or not?"

"Well, I don't know for sure, but Jesus said that the
Publican went down to his house justified. I suppose that
means that everyone who prays that prayer'll get God's
mercy."

Julius was a slow thinking man, and he mulled it over in
his mind. "Yes sir," he said. "I believe you're right." This
time he really prayed the prayer of the Publican. And when
he got to his feet the change in his soul was written in his
face. The features were the same, large and coarse, and the
wrinkles that made him look so hard and angry were still
there; but his eyes seemed to have caught fire from the
light in his soul, and the flame that burned there softened,

and transformed his face. There was a smile there as he thrust his hand into Jim's. "Thank you, son."

Martha was much better when they returned to the tent. She had no broken bones, and was resting easily. The doctor said that she would have to remain in bed for awhile; but, barring complications, she should be as well as ever in a few days.

Roy had a broken ankle and a severely lacerated scalp where his head had plowed into the sand as he pitched headlong off his horse. The doctor told Julius that he was in no danger, even though the pain was extreme.

John knew, the moment that Julius approached him, that he had *changed*. The big saloon owner couldn't speak. He took the Parson's hand and wrung it warmly, while the tears rolled down his cheeks.

Chapter 18

THE next morning before breakfast Julius Hart drove up to the Williams boarding house and called John outside.

"Would you like to go for a ride, Parson?"

"I don't know whether I ought to leave Martha," he said hesitantly.

"This is important. I thought we'd go down to North Platte and see what we could do for that kid they've got locked up down there. Gus Craig was my partner for ten years, and there wasn't a meaner disposition in the county. I think I might be able to help get young Morelin off."

"I reckon I can leave for that," John answered. "I want to go up and tell Martha good-by."

He got his hat and stepped quietly into the room.

"Hello, darling."

"I didn't know if you was awake."

"I've just been waiting for you to come in."

"How are you feeling this morning?"

She smiled. "I feel sort of stiff and sore, but I reckon I'll be up before you know it."

"You'd better be minding the doctor, or I'll have to turn you over my knee."

"I dare you to try it." Then she changed the subject abruptly. "Didn't I hear them talking about Jim's Paw last night?"

"Yes, I reckon you did. Everyone in town's talking about him. Jim led him to Christ last night."

"Oh, that's grand," she beamed. "That'll make everything so much nicer for Nancy and Jim."

"Now, Julius and I are going down to North Platte to see what we can do for Tom."

"I sure hope you can get him out. It'll be awful for that poor woman if he has to go to the penitentiary."

"We're going to do our best, but it'd probably be best not to say anything to Mrs. Morelin till we get back. There's no use fretting her about it."

"I won't."

"Good-by, dear."

"Aren't you going to kiss me?"

He complied gently.

"I thought you were saving that kind for an old maid aunt," she scolded. "Here." She pulled him close, pressing her warm, soft lips firmly against his own.

"Good-by, darling," he said again.

"Good-by," she replied. "I'll be praying for Tommy and his mother every single minute."

As John and Julius Hart rode out of town in the latter's springboard wagon, John looked over towards the Gold Eagle saloon.

"Who's looking after your business, Brother Hart?"

"Oh, I locked it up," he said offhandedly. "I don't see how a fellow could be in *that* business and be a Christian, too."

"I think you made a wise decision."

"Now I don't know what to do with it. I don't figure I can sell it to be used as a saloon, and I don't know what else could go in there. I think I'll go out on the ranch anyway." He pulled the team up short, and turned to John.

"Say, how'd you like to have that building for a church? Course I'd remodel it, and put in seats and stuff. I believe it'd do for awhile, anyway."

"Brother Hart," John said, his voice unsteady and quavering. "Of course it would do for a church, and we need a place to meet. I don't know how I can ever thank you."

"Don't thank me, thank God — and Jimmy." They rode along for several miles. It seemed to John that his companion didn't care to talk, so he remained silent. "I didn't sleep much last night, Parson," Hart began at last. "I think I'm about as black a sinner as ever found the Grace of God. How I'll ever right all the wrongs I did, I can't figure out."

"We all find ourselves in the same boat when it comes to sin. I reckon about the most we can do is just try to make up for it in Christian living, and to thank God that He'll take us, sin and all, and make us clean."

"I hated you, Parson, because I've been afraid of you and the Gospel you preach. I've been afraid of you ever since you changed Belle. I've been the cause of all your trouble here."

John grinned. "I've known that for a long time."

"But you didn't know that Gus and me stirred up all the trouble against the homesteaders. We drove critters through their fences, and trampled down their crops just to aggravate them, and we kept the ranchers all worked up with a bunch of lies. I made up other reasons to tell the men, but it was because I was feared that if the homesteaders stayed on, you'd stay, too."

At North Platte they talked with the county attorney. He knew Gus Craig, and wasn't anxious to press charges, but Julius insisted upon it.

The hearing was short. Tom told what had happened just prior to the shooting, and Julius Hart surprised everyone in the court room, except John, by testifying that Craig was an evil-tempered bully, and had boasted that he was going to scare the widow white-headed, and beat Tom within an inch of his life. When they finished, the jury foreman arose.

"We already got our minds made up," he said.

"I think you'd better go into the jury room anyway," the judge said. "Then we'll be in keepin' with the law."

"Well, all right, but it's just a waste of time." They filed out, and the last one had no sooner stepped out the door until they returned. "Now, as I was goin' to say," the foreman began. "We figure this kid shot Craig, like they said; but we don't see how anyone could blame him, considerin' how young he is, and how Craig was threatenin' his Maw. If we got anything to say about it, we're in favor of lettin' the boy go."

"Does-does that mean I'm free? That I can go home to my Maw?" Tom asked incredulously.

"Yes, my boy, it does. I agree with the jury. No court on earth would convict you on the evidence that was presented here."

On the way home Tom sat very still and quiet between the two men. His mother saw them when they pulled into the yard, and ran to the gate. At first she could scarcely believe that he was free, but when they assured her that no charges would be filed, she clasped him to her breast, and held him tight. Neither spoke until she lifted her eyes and murmured, "Thank God."

That evening before the meeting Jim and Nancy and the Parson were sitting in Martha's room beside her bed.

"You got to hurry and get well for the wedding," Nancy was saying.

"When's it going to be?"

"A week from next Wednesday."

"Oh, I'll be up and frisky as a colt by then."

"Jim's Paw is going to be the best man, and we'd like to have you be matron of honor."

"I'd think a fellow could just up an' get married without all that fuss and bother, wouldn't you, Parson?" Jim complained good-naturedly.

"It's a woman's world. I guess we'll just have to put up with it."

"Have you got a place to live yet?" Martha asked Nancy.

"Didn't we tell you? Jim's Paw is having us move in with him till we get our homestead fixed again. He's going to buy out Craig, and give Jim part of the ranch land and stock. Belle's going out to the ranch to keep house for him and Roy."

"How is Roy, anyway?"

"Oh, he'll be in bed for quite a spell, but the doctor thinks his ankle'll be as good as ever."

"We'll be seein' you folks after the meetin'," Jim said, going out the door behind Nancy. "You haven't been married for so long, but what you like to be alone once in awhile, anyway."

"Have you written to the Bishop?" Martha asked when the door was closed.

"I'm writing him tonight, and to the Superintendent, too. Isn't it grand, Martha? We've done what we set out to do. With God's help we've laid the foundation for our church.

Julius is giving his saloon building to be made into a church, and we're going to form the nucleus for the congregation tonight. With him helping instead of fighting us, it'll be easy."

"It's so wonderful, I can hardly believe it's all true."

"We've not only succeeded in our work, but I have you," he leaned close to her and took her hand. "And it won't be so very many months until we'll have our baby. If it's a girl, I hope she's as beautiful and sweet as her mother."

Martha kissed him again. "If we have a boy," she added, "I'm hoping that he's got a fighting heart, like his father, and that he uses it fighting for the Lord."

THE END